Jason
Merry Christmas 1974.
Happy Reading!
Love,
Uncle Bill, Aunt Elaine
and Katherine

FAVORITE CHRISTMAS STORIES

FAVORITE
CHRISTMAS STORIES

A Collection of Christmas Stories, Poems and Legends

Compiled by

FRANCES CAVANAH

Illustrated by

NELLIE H. FARNAM

GROSSET & DUNLAP • *Publishers*

NEW YORK

This book
is dedicated
to
Sammy and Jimmy

*F*oreword

There is so much that is old about Christmas. There is so much that is new. So in this book you will find stories both old and new—many so new they have never appeared in such a collection before. Others are old, for how can one imagine any group of holiday stories without Tiny Tim, "The Fir Tree," " 'Twas the Night Before Christmas" and—most important of all—the story of Jesus' birthday from the Bible!

But each story and poem, be it old or new, expresses in its own way the age-old spirit of Christmas. May you keep this spirit alive in your hearts and so keep it alive in a changing world! For it may be in this way the world will finally come to know the peace and good will of which the angels sang.

Frances Cavanah

"A story! A story!" the children cried, dragging a little fat man over toward the Tree. He sat down under it and said, "Now the Tree can listen, too."
—From "THE FIR TREE"
Hans Christian Andersen

Contents

	PAGE

THE OLD STORIES

'Twas the Night before Christmas*
......*Clement Clarke Moore*   3

Tiny Tim's Christmas............*Charles Dickens*   6

The Fir Tree............*Hans Christian Andersen*   13

THE BIRTHDAY OF JESUS

The Bible Story
......*According to Saint Matthew and Saint Luke*   27

A Christmas Carol............*G. K. Chesterton*   31

Christmas Gifts............*Marjorie Barrows*   33

The Friendly Beasts*......*Twelfth Century Carol*   34

The Christmas Rose......*Adapted by Lizzie Deas*   36

The Birthday............*Margaret E. Sangster*   38

The Stranger Child............*Count Franz Pocci*   53

O Little Town of Bethlehem......*Phillips Brooks*   58

CHRISTMAS IN THE OLD COUNTRIES

Yuletide Customs in Many Lands......*Lou Crandall*   61

Christmas Pantomime............*Hugh Walpole*   66
    A Story of England

Christmas Sheaves............*Nora Burglon*   81
    A Story of Norway

CHRISTMAS IN AMERICA

The First New England Christmas
......*Gertrude L. Stone and M. Grace Fickett*   95

* *For younger children*

[ix]

CONTENTS

PAGE

CHRISTMAS IN AMERICA—(Continued)

Little Girl of Long Ago*.........*Marjorie Barrows* 105

A Christmas Gift for the General
......*Jeannette Covert Nolan* 107
A Story of the Revolution

Sky-Fallen Peace.............*Josephine E. Phillips* 120
Christmas in the Northwest Territory

A Trade-About Christmas........*Frances Cavanah* 130
A Story of 1862

A Miserable, Merry Christmas......*Lincoln Steffens* 144
A Real Adventure in California in the Seventies

Born is the King of Israel.............*Ruth Sawyer* 152
An Old-Fashioned Christmas in New York

Christmas in the Street of Memories
......*Elizabeth Rhodes Jackson* 166
An Adventure in Boston

THE MAGIC OF CHRISTMAS

Pegasus and the Star...............*John Brangwyn* 183

The Christmas Masquerade
......*Mary E. Wilkins Freeman* 199

The Runaway Christmas Bus*..*Florence Page Jaques* 215

ALL ABOUT SANTA CLAUS

On Christmas Eve*...................*Stella Mead* 229

Santa Claus, a Wonder Story*.......*Maud Lindsay* 231

Behind the White Brick...*Frances Hodgson Burnett* 234

CHRISTMAS FUN AND NONSENSE

Lord Octopus Went to the Christmas Fair
......*Stella Mead* 251

The Peterkins' Christmas Tree......*Lucretia P. Hale* 253

Mrs. Goose's Wild Christmas*..*Miriam Clark Potter* 262

ACKNOWLEDGMENTS 273

ABOUT THE AUTHORS........................ 275

For younger children

[x]

THE OLD STORIES

'Twas the Night Before Christmas

Clement Clarke Moore

'Twas the night before Christmas, when all through the
    house
Not a creature was stirring, not even a mouse;
The stockings were hung by the chimney with care,
In hopes that St. Nicholas soon would be there.
The children were nestled all snug in their beds,
While visions of sugar plums danced in their heads;
And mama in her kerchief, and I in my cap,
Had just settled our brains for a long winter's nap,
When out on the lawn there arose such a clatter,
I sprang from my bed to see what was the matter.
Away to the window I flew like a flash,

Tore open the shutters and threw up the sash.
The moon on the breast of the new-fallen snow
Gave the luster of midday to objects below,
When, what to my wondering eyes should appear,
But a miniature sleigh, and eight tiny reindeer,
With a little old driver, so lively and quick,
I knew in a moment it must be Saint Nick.
More rapid than eagles his coursers they came,
And he whistled and shouted, and called them by name:
"Now, Dasher! now, Dancer! now, Prancer and Vixen!
On, Comet! on, Cupid! on, Donder and Blitzen!
To the top of the porch! to the top of the wall!
Now dash away! dash away! dash away all!"
As dry leaves that before the wild hurricane fly,
When they meet with an obstacle, mount to the sky,
So up to the housetop the coursers they flew,
With the sleigh full of toys, and St. Nicholas, too.
And then, in a twinkling, I heard on the roof
The prancing and pawing of each little hoof.
As I drew in my head, and was turning around,
Down the chimney St. Nicholas came with a bound.
He was dressed all in fur, from his head to his foot,
And his clothes were all covered with ashes and soot;
A bundle of toys he had flung on his back,
And he looked like a peddler just opening his pack.
His eyes, how they twinkled! his dimples, how merry!
His cheeks were like roses, his nose like a cherry!
His droll little mouth was drawn up like a bow,
And the beard on his chin was as white as the snow;
The stump of a pipe he held tight in his teeth,

And the smoke it encircled his head like a wreath;
He had a broad face and a little round belly
That shook, when he laughed, like a bowlful of jelly.
He was chubby and plump, a right jolly old elf,
And I laughed when I saw him, in spite of myself;
A wink of his eye and a twist of his head,
Soon gave me to know I had nothing to dread;
He spoke not a word, but went straight to his work,
And filled all the stockings; then turned with a jerk,
And laying his finger aside of his nose
And giving a nod, up the chimney he rose;
He sprang to his sleigh, to his team gave a whistle,
And away they all flew like the down of a thistle.
But I heard him exclaim, ere he drove out of sight,
"Happy Christmas to all, and to all a good night!"

Tiny Tim's Christmas

Charles Dickens

Then up rose Mrs. Cratchit, Cratchit's wife, dressed out but poorly in a twice-turned gown, but brave in ribbons, which are cheap and make a goodly show for sixpence; and she laid the cloth, assisted by Belinda Cratchit, second of her daughters, also brave in ribbons; while Master Peter Cratchit plunged a fork into the saucepan of potatoes, and getting the corners of his monstrous shirt collar (Bob's private property, conferred upon his son and heir in honor of the day) into his mouth, rejoiced to find himself so gallantly attired, and yearned to show his linen in the fashionable Parks. And now two smaller Cratchits, boy and girl, came tearing in, screaming that outside the baker's they had smelt the goose, and known it for their own; and basking in luxurious thoughts of sage and onion, these young Cratchits danced about the table, and exalted Master Peter Cratchit to the skies, while he (not proud, although his collars nearly choked him) blew the fire, until the slow potatoes bubbling up, knocked loudly at the saucepan lid to be let out and peeled.

"What has ever got your precious father, then?" said Mrs. Cratchit. "And your brother, Tiny Tim! And Martha warn't as late last Christmas Day by half-an-hour!"

"Here's Martha, mother!" said a girl, appearing as she spoke.

"Here's Martha, mother!" cried the two young Cratchits. "Hurrah! There's *such* a goose, Martha!"

"Why, bless your heart alive, my dear, how late you are!" said Mrs. Cratchit, kissing her a dozen times, and taking off her shawl and bonnet for her with officious zeal.

"We'd a deal of work to finish up last night," replied the girl, "and had to clear away this morning, mother!"

"Well! Never mind so long as you are come," said Mrs. Cratchit. "Sit ye down before the fire, my dear, and have a warm, Lord bless ye!"

"No, no! There's father coming," cried the two young Cratchits, who were everywhere at once. "Hide, Martha, hide!"

So Martha hid herself, and in came little Bob, the

father, with at least three feet of comforter exclusive of the fringe, hanging down before him; and his threadbare clothes darned up and brushed, to look seasonable; and Tiny Tim upon his shoulder. Alas for Tiny Tim, he bore a little crutch, and had his limbs supported by an iron frame!

"Why, where's our Martha?" cried Bob Cratchit, looking round.

"Not coming," said Mrs. Cratchit.

"Not coming!" said Bob, with a sudden declension in his high spirits; for he had been Tim's blood horse all the way from church, and had come home rampant. "Not coming upon Christmas Day!"

Martha didn't like to see him disappointed, if it were only in joke; so she came out prematurely from behind the closet door, and ran into his arms, while the two young Cratchits hustled Tiny Tim, and bore him off into the wash-house, that he might hear the pudding singing in the copper.

"And how did little Tim behave?" asked Mrs. Cratchit, when she had rallied Bob on his credulity, and Bob had hugged his daughter to his heart's content.

"As good as gold," said Bob, "and better. Somehow, he gets thoughtful, sitting by himself so much, and thinks the strangest things you ever heard. He told me, coming home, that he hoped the people saw him in the church, because he was a cripple, and it might be pleasant to them to remember upon Christmas Day, who made lame beggars walk, and blind men see."

Bob's voice was tremulous when he told them this,

and trembled more when he said that Tiny Tim was growing strong and hearty.

His active little crutch was heard upon the floor, and back came Tiny Tim before another word was spoken, escorted by his brother and sister to his stool before the fire; and while Bob, turning up his cuffs— as if, poor fellow, they were capable of being made more shabby—compounded some hot mixture in a jug with gin and lemons, and stirred it round and round and put it on the hob to simmer; Master Peter, and the two ubiquitous young Cratchits went to fetch the goose, with which they soon returned in high procession.

Such a bustle ensued that you might have thought a goose the rarest of all birds; a feathered phenomenon, to which a black swan was a matter of course—and in truth it was something very like it in that house. Mrs. Cratchit made the gravy (ready beforehand in a little saucepan) hissing hot; Master Peter mashed the potatoes with incredible vigor; Miss Belinda sweetened up the apple-sauce; Martha dusted the hot plates; Bob took Tiny Tim beside him in a tiny corner at the table; the two young Cratchits set chairs for everybody, not forgetting themselves, and mounting guard upon their posts, crammed spoons into their mouths, lest they should shriek for goose before their turn came to be helped. At last the dishes were set on, and grace was said. It was succeeded by a breathless pause, as Mrs. Cratchit, looking slowly all along the carving knife, prepared to plunge it in the breast; but when she did, and when the long expected gush of stuffing issued forth, one murmur of delight arose all around the board, and even Tiny Tim, excited by the two young Cratchits, beat on the table with the handle of his knife, and feebly cried Hurrah!

There never was such a goose. Bob said he didn't believe there ever was such a goose cooked. Its tenderness and flavor, size and cheapness, were the themes of universal admiration. Eked out by apple-sauce and mashed potatoes, it was a sufficient dinner for the whole family; indeed, as Mrs. Cratchit said with great delight (surveying one small atom of a bone upon the dish), they hadn't ate it all at last! Yet every one had had enough, and the youngest Cratchits in particular, were steeped in sage and onion to the eyebrows! But now, the plates being changed by Miss Belinda, Mrs. Cratchit left the room alone—too nervous to bear witnesses—to take the pudding up and bring it in.

Suppose it should not be done enough! Suppose it should break in turning out! Suppose somebody should have got over the wall of the backyard, and stolen it, while they were merry with the goose—a supposition at which the two young Cratchits became livid! All sorts of horrors were supposed.

Hallo! A great deal of steam! The pudding was out of the copper. A smell like a washing-day! That was the cloth.A smell like an eating-house and a pastry-cook's next door to each other, with a laundress's next door to that! That was the pudding! In half a minute Mrs. Cratchit entered—flushed, but smiling proudly—with the pudding, like a speckled cannon-ball, so hard and firm, blazing in half of half-a-quartern of ignited brandy, and bedight with Christmas holly stuck into the top.

Oh, a wonderful pudding! Bob Cratchit said, and calmly too, that he regarded it as the greatest success achieved by Mrs. Cratchit since their marriage. Mrs. Cratchit said that now the weight was off her mind, she would confess she had had her doubts about the quantity of flour. Everybody had something to say about it, but nobody said or thought it was at all a small pudding for a large family. It would have been flat heresy to do so. Any Cratchit would have blushed to hint at such a thing.

At last the dinner was all done, the cloth was cleared, the hearth swept, and the fire made up. The compound in the jug being tasted, and considered perfect, apples and oranges were put upon the table, and a shovelful of chestnuts on the fire. Then all the Cratchit family drew round the hearth, in what Bob Cratchit called a circle, meaning half a one; and at Bob Cratchit's elbow stood the family display of glass. Two tumblers, and a custard-cup without a handle.

These held the hot stuff from the jug, however, as well as golden goblets would have done; and Bob served it out with beaming looks, while the chestnuts on the fire sputtered and cracked noisily. Then Bob proposed:

"A Merry Christmas to us all, my dears. God bless us!"

Which all the family re-echoed.

"God bless us every one!" said Tiny Tim, the last of all.

The Fir Tree

Retold from Hans Christian Andersen

Once upon a time there was a pretty, green little Fir Tree. The sun shone on him; he had plenty of fresh air; and around him grew many large comrades, pines as well as firs. But the little Fir was not satisfied. He did not think of the sun and the fresh air. He wanted to be a big tree like the others.

Sometimes the little children living in the cottages near by came into the woods looking for wild strawberries. They ran about, laughing and talking, and often they brought a whole pitcher full of berries, or a long row of them threaded on a straw, and sat down near the young Tree. "Oh, what a nice little Fir!" they said. But the Tree did not like to hear them talk this way. He did not like to be called "little."

By the time he was a year old he had grown a good deal. Another year passed and he was another long bit taller. With a fir tree one can tell by the number of shoots it has how old it is. "Oh, if I were only as tall as the other trees," he thought. "Then I could spread out my branches and look out into the wide world. The birds would build nests in my branches; and when there was a breeze I could bend with a stately bow like the others."

The Tree sighed, taking no pleasure in the sunbeams and the birds and the red clouds, which morning and evening, sailed above him.

In the wintertime, when the snow lay white and glittering on the ground, a hare would often come leaping along. Sometimes he jumped over the little Tree, and that made him very angry. But by the third winter the Tree had grown so large the hare had to go around it. That made the Tree feel better. "The most delightful thing in the world," he thought, "is to grow and grow and be tall and old."

In autumn the woodcutters came and cut down some of the largest trees. This happened every year and the little Fir Tree, which was not so little any more, was frightened. How he trembled as the magnificent trees fell to the earth with a great noise and crackling. After the branches had been lopped off, the trees looked so long and bare that it was hard to recognize them. Then they were laid in carts, and the horses dragged them out of the woods.

"What becomes of them?" the Fir Tree wondered.

In spring, when the Swallows and the Storks came, the Tree said to them, "Do you know where they have been taken?"

The Swallows did not know anything about it, but one of the Storks nodded his head thoughtfully. "I think I know," he said. "As I was flying hither from Egypt, I met many ships with tall masts and they smelt of fir. You may feel proud of them, so majestic did they look."

"If I were only old enough to fly across the ocean!" sighed the Tree. "How does the ocean look? What is it like?"

"That would take a long time to explain," said the Stork, and off he flew.

"Rejoice in thy youth!" said the Sunbeams. "Rejoice in thy growth!" And the Wind kissed the Tree, the Dew wept tears over him; but the Fir did not understand.

When Christmas came, many young trees were cut down. Some of them were neither so large nor so old as the Fir Tree, but they were always the finest looking. Their branches were left on them when they were laid carefully on the carts, and the horses drew them out of the woods.

"They are no taller than I," complained the Fir Tree. "Indeed one of them was much shorter. Why are they allowed to keep all their branches? Where are they going?"

"We know! We know!" twittered the Sparrows. "We have peeped in at the windows in the town below! We saw the trees planted in the middle of the warm rooms and ornamented with the most splendid things— with gilded apples, with gingerbread, with toys and hundreds of lights!"

A tremor ran through the Fir Tree. "And then? What happens after that?"

"We did not see anything more, but it was very beautiful."

"Ah, perhaps I shall know the same brightness some day," the Tree rejoiced. "That would be better than to cross the ocean. If Christmas would only come! I am as tall as the trees that were carried off last year. My branches spread as far. Oh, if I were only on the cart now! If I were only in the warm room with all the splendor and magnificence! Something better, something still grander, is sure to follow—but what? How I long, how I suffer! I wonder what is the matter with me!"

"Rejoice in us!" said the Air and the Sunlight. "Rejoice in thy own youth!"

But the Tree did not rejoice. He grew and grew. He was green both winter and summer. "What a fine tree!" people said, and toward Christmas he was one of the first to be cut down. The ax struck deep, and the Tree fell to earth with a sigh. He was not happy; he could only think how sad it was to be taken away from the place where he had sprung up. He knew that never again would he see his dear old comrades, the little bushes and flowers around him; perhaps he would never even see the birds again. And he didn't like it at all.

The Tree was laid on a cart with several others and taken away. When he came to himself again he was being unloaded in a big yard, and two servants in handsome livery carried him into a large and beautiful drawing room. Here there were portraits hanging on the walls and, near the white porcelain stove, two big Chinese vases with lions on the covers. There were big easy chairs, silken cushions and tables filled with picture books and toys. The Fir Tree was stuck upright in a tub filled with sand; but it did not look like a tub, for green cloth was hung all around it and it stood on a large, bright carpet.

A tremor ran through the Tree. What was going to happen? Several young ladies decorated it, aided by the servants. On one branch they hung little nets made of colored paper and filled with sugar plums. On the other boughs they hung gilded apples and walnuts which looked as though they had grown there. Then little blue and white and red candles were fastened to the branches. Among the foliage there were dolls which looked like people—the Tree had never seen anything like them before—and at the very top there was a large star of gold tinsel. It was really splendid—too splendid for any words to describe.

"Just wait till evening!" everybody said. "How the Tree will shine this evening!"

"Oh, if evening would only come!" thought the Tree. "If the candles were only lighted! What will happen then, I wonder. Will the other trees from the forest come to look at me? Will the sparrows beat against the windowpanes? Perhaps I shall take root and stand here winter and summer covered with ornaments!" He grew so impatient that he got a pain in his bark, and this with trees is the same as a headache with us.

When at last the candles were lighted, there was such brightness, such splendor, the Tree trembled in every bough. One of the candles set fire to the foliage, and it blazed up splendidly.

"Help! Help!" cried the young ladies and rushed to put out the fire.

After that the Tree did not dare tremble. He was quite bewildered by the glare and the brightness. Suddenly both the folding doors opened, and in rushed the children, with the older persons following more quietly. The little ones stood quite still, but only for a moment. Then they shouted for joy, and the room echoed with their shouts. They began dancing around the Tree, pulling off one present after another.

"What are they doing?" thought the Tree. "What is to happen now?"

The candles burned down to the very branches, and as they burned down they were put out, one after another. Then the children were given permission to plunder the Tree, and they rushed upon it so violently that all its branches cracked. Then the children went on playing with their beautiful toys. No one even looked at the Tree, except the old nurse, who peeped in among the branches to see if there was a fig or an apple that had been overlooked.

"A story! A story!" the children cried, dragging a little fat man over toward the Tree. He sat down under it and said, "Now the Tree can listen, too. I shall tell you only one story, so which will you have: the one about Ivedy-Avedy, or the one about Klumpy-Dumpy who fell downstairs and yet married the princess and came to the throne after all?"

"Ivedy-Avedy!" cried some. "Klumpy-Dumpy!" cried others. There was a great deal of squealing, and finally the man told about Klumpy-Dumpy and the children clapped their hands and cried, "Go on! Go on!" The Fir Tree stood quite still, thinking: "Who knows? Perhaps I shall fall downstairs, too, and marry a princess!" And he looked forward to the next day, when he hoped to be decked out again with lights and toys and bright tinsel.

"I won't tremble tomorrow," he thought. "Tomorrow I shall hear again the story of Klumpy-Dumpy and perhaps that of Ivedy-Avedy, too." And all night long the Tree stood quite still, thinking.

The next morning in came the servants.

"Ah, now the splendor will begin again!" thought the Fir.

But no. The servants dragged him out of the room, up the stairs into the attic and there, in a dark corner, they left him. "What can this mean?" wondered the Tree, and he leaned against the wall lost in thought. And he had plenty of time for thinking. Days and nights passed and nobody came near him. When at last some-body did come up to the attic, it was only to leave some trunks. There stood the Tree quite hidden. There stood the Tree quite forgotten.

"It is winter out-of-doors!" he thought. "The earth is hard and covered with snow. I could not be planted now. These people are really very kind. They have put me up here under shelter until spring comes! If only it were not so dark and lonely here! Not even a hare! I liked it out in the woods when the snow was on the ground and the hare leaped by; yes, even when he jumped over me. Ah, but I did not like it then."

"Squeak, squeak!" said a little Mouse, peeping out of his hole. Then another little Mouse came and they sniffed at the Fir Tree and ran in and out among the branches.

"It is dreadfully cold," said the Mouse. "Except for that, it would be nice here, wouldn't it, old Fir?"

"I am not old," said the Fir Tree. "There is many a tree much older than I."

"Where do you come from?" asked the Mice. "Tell us about the most beautiful place in the world. Have

you ever been there? Have you ever been in the larder where there are cheeses lying on the shelves and hams hanging from the ceiling, where one may dance on tallow candles; a place where one goes in lean and comes out fat?"

"I know of no such place," said the Tree. "But I know the woods where the sun shines and the birds sing." Then he told of the time when he was young, and the little Mice had never heard the like before.

"How much you have seen!" they said. "How happy you must have been!"

"I?" said the Fir Tree, thinking it over. "Yes, those really were happy times." Then he told about Christmas Eve, when he had been decked out with beautiful ornaments and candles.

"Oh," said the little Mice. "How lucky you have been, old Fir Tree."

"I am not old," said he. "I came from the woods only this winter."

"But what wonderful stories you know!" said the Mice, and the next night they came with four other little Mice who wanted to hear the stories also. The more the Fir Tree talked about his youth, the more plainly he remembered it himself, and he realized that those times had really been very happy times. "But they may come again. Klumpy-Dumpy fell downstairs and yet he married a princess," said the Fir Tree. And at that moment he remembered a little birch tree growing out in the woods. To the Fir she seemed like a princess.

"Who is Klumpy-Dumpy?" asked the Mice. So the Fir Tree told the story, and the little Mice were so pleased they jumped to the very top of the Tree. The next night two more Mice came, and on Sunday two Rats. But they said the stories were not interesting. This worried the little Mice. They began to think the stories not very interesting either.

"Is that the only story you know?" asked the Rats.

"Only that one," said the Tree. "I heard it on the happiest night of my life; only then I did not know how happy I was."

"It's a silly story. Don't you know one about bacon and tallow candles? Can't you tell any larder stories?"

"No," said the Tree.

"Then good-by," said the Rats and went home.

At last the little Mice stopped coming, and the Tree sighed. "After all I liked having the sleek little Mice listen to my stories, but that is over now. When I am brought out again I am going to enjoy myself."

But when was that to be? Why, one morning a

number of people came up to the attic. Trunks were moved and the Tree was pulled out and thrown down on the floor. Then a man drew him toward the stairs, where the sun shone.

"Now life begins again," thought the Tree. He felt the fresh air, the first sunbeam—and then he was out in the yard. Everything happened so quickly he quite forgot to look to himself. The yard was right next to a garden where fragrant roses hung over the fence and lindens were in bloom. The Swallows flew by and said, "Quirre-vit! My husband is come!" But it was not the Fir Tree that they meant.

"Now I shall enjoy life," said he joyfully, and spread out his branches. But alas, they were all withered and yellow. He lay in a corner among weeds and nettles. The golden tinsel star was still on the tree, and it glittered in the sunlight.

In the yard some children were playing—the same children who had danced around the Fir Tree at Christmas time. They were glad to see him again, and the youngest child ran up and tore off the golden star.

"Look, what is still on the ugly old Christmas tree!" said he. And he trampled on the branches, so that they cracked beneath his feet.

The Tree looked at the beautiful garden and then at himself. He wished he had stayed in his dark corner in the loft. He thought of his youth in the woods, of the merry Christmas Eve, and of the little Mice who had listened so eagerly to the story of Klumpy-Dumpy.

" 'Tis over," said the poor Tree. "Had I but been

happy when I had reason to be! But 'tis all over now."

Then the gardener's boy chopped the Tree into small pieces, and the wood flamed up splendidly under a large brewing kettle. It sighed deeply, and each sigh was like a shot.

The children went on playing in the yard. On his chest the youngest wore the gold star which the Tree had had on the happiest evening of his life. But that was over now—the Tree gone, the story finished. Everything was over; every tale must come to an end at last.

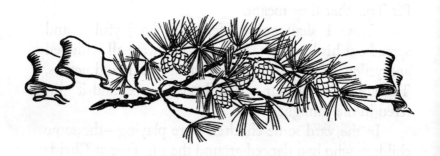

THE BIRTHDAY OF JESUS

The Bible Story

Based on the Saint Matthew Version

Now the birth of Jesus Christ was on this wise. Behold, the angel of the Lord appeared unto Joseph in a dream, saying, Joseph, thou son of David, fear not to take unto thee Mary thy wife, for she shall bring forth a son, and thou shalt call his name Jesus: for he shall save his people from their sins.

Then Joseph, being raised from sleep, did as the angel of the Lord had bidden him.

Now when Jesus was born in Bethlehem of Judaea in the days of Herod the king, behold there came three wise men from the east to Jerusalem, saying, Where is he that is born King of the Jews? for we have seen his star in the east, and are come to worship him.

When Herod the king had heard these things, he was troubled, and all Jerusalem with him. And when he had gathered the chief priests and scribes of the people together, he demanded of them where Christ should be born. They said unto him, In Bethlehem.

Then Herod, when he had privily called the wise men, inquired of them diligently what time the star appeared, and he sent them to Bethlehem and said, Go and search diligently for the young child, and when ye have found him bring me word again, that I also may come and worship him.

When they had heard the king they departed; and lo, the star went before them, till it came and stood over where the young child was. When they saw the star they rejoiced with exceeding great joy, and when they were come into the house they saw the young child with Mary his mother, and fell down, and worshiped him, and presented unto him gifts: gold, and frankincense, and myrrh.

Being warned of God in a dream that they should not return to Herod, they departed into their own country another way; and behold, the angel of the Lord appeareth to Joseph in a dream, saying, Arise, take the young child and his mother, and flee into Egypt, and be thou there until I bring thee word, for Herod will seek the young child to destroy him. When he arose he took the young child and his mother by night, and departed into Egypt . . .

*   *   *   *   *

Based on the Saint Luke Version

It came to pass in those days that there went out a decree from Caesar Augustus that all the world should be taxed, and Joseph went up from Nazareth unto Bethlehem to be taxed with Mary his wife. So it was that, while they were there, she brought forth her first-born son, and wrapped him in swaddling clothes, and laid him in a manger, because there was no room for them in the inn.

There were in the same country shepherds abiding in the field, keeping watch over their flock by night. And, lo, the angel of the Lord came upon them, and the glory of the Lord shone round about them; and they were sore afraid. And the angel said unto them, Fear not, for behold, I bring you good tidings of great joy, which shall be to all people, for unto you is born this day in the city of David a Saviour which is Christ the Lord. And this shall be a sign unto you: ye shall find the babe wrapped in swaddling clothes, lying in a manger.

Suddenly there was with the angel a multitude of the heavenly host, praising God, and saying, *Glory to God in the highest, and on earth peace, good will toward men.*

And it came to pass, as the angels were gone away from them into heaven, the shepherds said one to another, Let us now go unto Bethlehem, and see this which is to come to pass; and they came with haste, and found Mary and Joseph, and the babe lying in a manger. When they had seen it they made known abroad the saying which was told them concerning this child, and they that heard it wondered. But Mary kept all these things, and pondered them in her heart.

And the shepherds returned, glorifying and praising God for all the things they had heard and seen, as it was told unto them.

A Christmas Carol

G. K. Chesterton

The Christ Child lay on Mary's lap,
His hair was like a light.
(O weary, weary were the world,
But here is all aright.)

The Christ Child lay on Mary's breast,
His hair was like a star.
(O stern and cunning are the Kings,
But here the true hearts are.)

The Christ Child lay on Mary's heart,
His hair was like a fire.
(O weary, weary is the world,
But here the world's desire.)

The Christ Child stood at Mary's knee,
His hair was like a crown,
And all the flowers looked up at Him
And all the stars looked down.

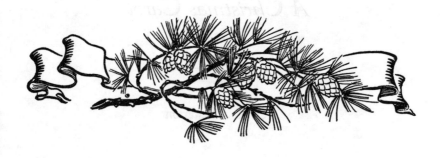

Christmas Gifts

Marjorie Barrows

The night was cool, the night was still,
    The desert sand was soft and white,
And there were stars up in the sky
    And one was bright.

And silently it shone upon
    The Wise Men as they rode along,
While in their hearts the Wise Men sang
    A Christmas song.

And when they reached the manger, there
    Was Mary with her new-born child,
And when He saw His gifts, I'm sure
    The Baby smiled.

The Friendly Beasts
Twelfth Century Carol

Jesus our brother, strong and good,
Was humbly born in a stable rude,
And the friendly beasts around Him stood,
Jesus our brother, strong and good.

"I," said the donkey, shaggy and brown,
"I carried His mother up hill and down,
"I carried her safely to Bethlehem town;
"I," said the donkey, shaggy and brown.

"I," said the cow all white and red,
"I gave Him my manger for His bed,
"I gave Him my hay to pillow His head,
"I," said the cow all white and red.

THE FRIENDLY BEASTS

"I," said the sheep with curly horn,
"I gave Him my wool for His blanket warm,
"He wore my coat on Christmas morn;
"I," said the sheep with curly horn.

"I," said the dove, from the rafters high,
"Cooed Him to sleep, my mate and I,
"We cooed Him to sleep, my mate and I;
"I," said the dove, from the rafters high.

And every beast, by some good spell,
In the stable dark was glad to tell,
Of the gift he gave Immanuel,
The gift he gave Immanuel.

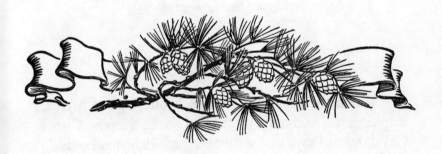

The Christmas Rose
An Old Legend

Lizzie Deas (Adapted)

When the Magi laid their rich offerings of myrrh, frankincense, and gold, by the bed of the sleeping Christ Child, legend says that a shepherd maiden stood outside the door quietly weeping.

She, too, had sought the Christ Child. She, too, desired to bring him gifts. But she had nothing to offer, for she was very poor indeed. In vain she had searched the countryside over for one little flower to bring Him, but she could find neither bloom nor leaf, for the winter had been cold.

And as she stood there weeping, an angel passing saw her sorrow, and stooping he brushed aside the snow at her feet. And there sprang up on the spot a cluster of beautiful winter roses—waxen white with pink-tipped petals.

"Nor myrrh, nor frankincense, nor gold," said the angel, "is offering more meet for the Christ Child than these pure Christmas Roses."

Joyfully the shepherd maiden gathered the flowers and made her offering to the Holy Child.

The Birthday

Margaret E. Sangster

The boy sat quite alone on the hilltop, his shepherd's crook across his knees, his small square lunch basket beside him. He made an odd, distorted shadow in the white light of the moon, for even the fringed shawl that his mother had woven of lamb's wool could not hide the ugly hump that lay—a burden much too heavy for so young a lad to bear—between his shoulders.

Far below him, dotting the hillside with other irregular shadows, were the sheep. The majority of them slept, but a few wandered aimlessly up and down the slope. The boy, however, was not watching the flock.

His head was thrown back, and his wide eyes were fixed on the sky.

"Perhaps it will happen again," he was thinking, "perhaps—though a third of a century has gone by. Perhaps I shall see the great star and hear the angel voices as my father did!"

The moon, riding high in the heavens, went under a blanket of cloud. For a moment the world was dark. The boy sighed and lowered his eyes.

"It is an omen," he breathed, "an omen! Though it is the time of anniversary, there will be no star this night. Neither will the angels sing . . ."

The time of anniversary. How often the boy had listened to the story of the miracle that had taken place so long ago! The boy's father had been a lad himself then—he had been the youngest of the shepherds on that glorious occasion when an angel anthem sounded across the world and a star shone above the tranquil town of Bethlehem. The boy's father had followed the star; with the other shepherds he had come to the stable of the inn. Crowding through the narrow doorway, he had seen a woman with a baby in her arms.

"But—" the boy's father had told the story so many times that his family and the neighbors knew it word for word—"she was no ordinary woman! There was something in her face that made one think of a lighted candle. And there was a tenderness in her smile that the very cattle felt, for they drew close to her and seemed to kneel. It was not her beauty, although beauty she did possess! It was a shine from within——"

"And the baby—" the boy always prompted his father here—*"what of the baby?"*

The father's hand touched his small son's shoulder at this point—touched it, and drew away.

"The baby," he said, and his voice grew hushed, "was as unlike other infants as his mother was different from other women. Scarce an hour old when first I glimpsed him, there was a sense of wisdom—no, do not laugh—on his brow, and his tiny up-curled hands seemed —indeed, I do mean it!—to hold power. I found myself kneeling, as the cattle knelt, and there was the damp of tears upon my face, and—though I was a lad tall for my age—I was not ashamed."

Alone on the hillside the boy could almost hear the sound of his father's voice in the stillness. His father's voice telling the story of the marvelous infant and of the Wise Men who had come to the stable—following, also, in the path of the star. They had come bearing gifts, the fame of which traveled through all the land. Often the boy had heard of the gold and frankincense and myrrh; often he had shivered at the tale of the great cruel king who had ordered death to all male infants. Often he had thrilled to the saga of a worried young mother—and her sober husband—who had stolen away into the land of Egypt with her child.

"Many of us thought," the boy's father finished, "that the child had been captured and slain by Herod. Until a decade passed and we heard rumors of a youth who bore his name, and who lectured in a temple at Jerusalem to a group of learned doctors. A few years

ago we heard that this same youth, grown older, had organized a band of men, that with them he was journeying from place to place, preaching and teaching and aiding the needy. And—" here the boy's father had a habit of lowering his voice and glancing furtively around the room—"there are some who say that he has become a Messiah, and that he does more than champion the cause of the common people. There are some who say that he performs wonderful deeds, healing the halt and the blind and the lepers—even raising the dead."

Once, at this point, the boy interrupted. "I would that I might meet him," he had said with ill-masked eagerness. "I would that he might take the hump from my back and make me strong and straight like other children."

It was growing cold on the hillside. The child drew

the shawl closer about his tired body and wished that he were not a shepherd. Shepherds led a lonely life—they did not fit into the bright places of the world. Rooms gaily lighted at eventide were for the men and boys who worked hard by day and earned their moments of ease; they were not for shepherds. But what else could a crippled lad do to justify his existence—what else than tend sheep? A crippled lad who could not undertake physical labor and who had no talents.

Yawning wearily, the boy glanced at the sky. From the position of the moon he judged it to be middle night —it was still a long while before sunrise; still hours before someone would come to take his place and he could limp home. And yet middle night had its compensations! For at that time he could break his fast and partake of the lunch that his mother had packed so neatly into a basket.

As he reached for the basket, as he opened it slowly, the boy was wondering what had been prepared for his refreshment. He found, to his satisfaction, that there was a flask of goat's milk, and nearly a loaf of crusty dark bread, and some yellow cheese; that there were dried figs, sugary with their own sweetness. And, wrapped separately, he came upon a real treat. A cake made of eggs and sifted flour, with citron in it, and raisins!

He had expected the bread and the cheese and the milk. Even the figs he had expected. But the cake was a surprise, the sort of surprise that happened seldom. His eyes gleamed as he surveyed it, and some of the sadness went out of them. Carefully he set the basket down and spread on the ground beside him the square of linen in which his mother had folded the lunch. Carefully he laid out the flask of milk, the bread, the cheese—but not the cake, which he left tucked away in the depths of the basket. He left it there so that he might not be tempted to eat it first!

"It is good to be hungry," he said aloud. "Yes—and to have food!"

From somewhere just behind him a voice spoke. It was not a loud voice, and yet the music of it seemed to carry beyond the hillside.

"Indeed, yes!" said the voice. "It is good to be hungry. And to have food, and to——"

Startled, for he had thought he was quite alone with his thoughts and the drowsing sheep, the boy glanced back across his crooked shoulder. He saw a man standing upon the brow of the hill, silhouetted against the night sky. Ordinarily he would have known fear, for there were cruel robbers abroad often at middle night. But somehow the sight of this man, who was tall and muscular, failed to frighten him. He did not know why he instinctively completed the man's unfinished sentence.

"And to share it!" he murmured, as if in a dream. "You are a stranger, sir?"

The man came closer to the child and stood looking down upon him. "No, not a stranger," he said slowly, "never a stranger. As it happens, my journey started not far from this very place—started years before you, my lad, saw the light. I am by way of completing a circle."

Although he couldn't imagine what the man meant, the boy made swift response.

"I was about to eat my lunch," he said, indicating the square of linen on which he had arranged the contents of his basket. "One grows ravenous on the hillside. I am a shepherd, sir. I tend my father's flock, and each night my mother packs for me a simple repast. Will you be seated—you who have journeyed so long—and break bread with me? Perhaps—" he hesitated shyly—"you will talk with me as we eat? It grows lonely on the dark hillside—I pine at times for companionship."

The man continued to peer down from his impressive height. His eyes held a warm glow—it was as if a candle burned somewhere behind them, the boy thought, and remembered words that his father had spoken when he described a woman in a stable. He felt so comforted by the man's glance that he smiled up into the kindly face, and the man spoke again.

"It is a strange coincidence," he said, "the fact that you are a shepherd, for I also tend my father's flock! And I also—" his smile was luminous—"have often grown lonely waiting for the gates of dawn to open. Are you sure—" he seated himself upon the ground— "that you have enough for two? I should not like to deprive you of anything."

Gazing, fascinated, into the man's face, the boy replied:

"But, yes! I have a large flask of goat's milk, and some yellow cheese, and nearly a loaf of bread, and ten figs. And—" for a second he hesitated—"that's a great plenty," he finished lamely. He did not mention the cake, still wrapped in the basket. For a cake—a cake made of sifted flour and eggs and citron and raisins—was a rare delicacy. And it was not a very big cake.

The man bent forward to retie the thong of a sandal. The boy saw that the sandal was covered with dust. He tried to keep his eyes from glancing toward his lunch basket as he tore the crusty dark bread into fragments.

"Perhaps your feet are aching," he ventured as he placed the fragments in the center of the linen cloth. "This hill is hard to climb. I am close to being spent when I reach the summit of it, but I must needs sit high so that I can watch all the sheep."

The man said slowly: "I have climbed steeper hills than this one, my lad, and know that there are steeper hills to be. My feet do not ache. How long—" abruptly he changed the subject—"have you been crippled?"

Had it come from an ordinary person, the boy would have resented such a display of curiosity. From this man the question seemed a natural one, to be answered naturally.

"Why," he said, "I have never been without a hump between my shoulders. I hate it, but—" he was quoting his mother—"what must be, must be! Still—" his childish face was a trifle unchildish—"it is hard to go through life looking like one of the camels that the Wise Men rode when they came from the east with their caravans——"

The man interrupted. "What, lad," he queried, "do

you know of the Wise Men from the east? How does it happen that you should mention them to me on this night? It is—" he bit into a piece of the crusty dark bread—"very curious!"

Laughing softly, the little boy answered. "I suppose the Wise Men are in my mind," he said, "because this is the time of anniversary, and I have been thinking of the baby that was born in a stable. I was hoping—before you arrived—that once again the great star might shine and that the angels might sing. I have, in fact, been watching the sky rather than the sheep."

The man asked another swift question. "What," he queried, "do you know about these holy things—about the star and the song? You are so very young!"

The boy explained. "All Bethlehem," he said, "heard about the star, and about the infant who lay in the manger because there was no room at the inn. I know, perhaps, more than the others, for my father—a child then himself—was one of the shepherds who saw the light from the heavens and heard the angel music . . . Will you—" the boy had taken the flask of goat's milk into his hands—"will you share with me this cup, sir! For perhaps you thirst?"

The man took the flask from the fragile hands. His fingers were powerful and sinewy, but as gentle as a woman's. He said,

"I will share the cup with you, my lad, for I do thirst."

As he watched the man drinking deeply, the boy thought, "It must be tiring to tramp from place to place."

He said on impulse, as the stranger set down the flask, "Will you tell me, sir, of some of the towns in which you have stayed?"

The man answered: "One town is very like another, my lad, with poverty and pain rubbing elbows against wealth, with greed taking toll, all too often, of humanity. With health on one side and illness on the other. With so few gracious deeds that one can do to help the sore distressed—" he turned his face away—"and a lifetime in which to do them so desperately short!"

In a low tone the boy said: "Sometimes, when I was a tot, I hoped that my life might be short, but already I am ten years old. How old, sir, are you? I feel older than my years . . ."

The man's voice was muted as he replied, "I am more than three times your age, lad, but I, too, feel older than my years."

"You shouldn't, because you're so strong," the boy exclaimed. "When is your time of birth, sir? I was born when it was spring."

The man smiled his beautiful, luminous smile. "It's odd that you should ask, dear lad," he murmured, "for this is my day of birth. You, quite unknowing, are giving me an anniversary feast—and never has a feast been more welcome. I was weary and forlorn when I came upon you."

Weary and forlorn! As he stared at the man, the little boy queried:

"Haven't you any people of your own? People with whom you can make merry on your day of birth? When my birthday arrives, Mother prepares a *real* feast for me, and gives me gifts. This shawl I wear she wove for my last birthday. The year before she pressed a sheaf of bright flowers into wax. Once, when I was smaller, she made wondrous sweetmeats of honey and grain."

The man reached over and rested his hand on the little boy's knee. "I fear," he said, "that I have grown too old and large for birthday gifts. Furthermore, my loved ones are not near enough just now to make merry with me. But maybe, who knows, there will be a gift for me at my journey's end."

The boy's knee felt all atingle under the pressure of the friendly hand. He asked, "When, sir, will you come to your journey's end?"

The man did not meet the child's gaze. He replied, "Perhaps very soon!"

The boy was worried. He said: "You don't look happy about it. Don't you want to come to the end of your travels? Don't you want to reach home and see what gift they have in store for you?"

The man hesitated ever so slightly. "Yes," he said at last, "I want to reach—home. But the gift—it may be too beautiful to bear. Or too heavy for me to carry. I suppose—" his face looked drawn in the white moonlight—"I should be getting on. You have made this birthday very sweet, my lad!"

Peeping down at the white cloth with its remnants of bread and cheese, the boy thought: "There seems to be as much food as ever! He couldn't have liked it." Suddenly he was swept by a burning sense of shame. He spoke impetuously, one word tumbling over the other.

"You did not enjoy your food," he said, "and you have had no true birthday feast. That—though you have no way of guessing—is because I have been selfish and mean! I," he gulped out his confession, "have a cake in my basket—a cake that I was saving to eat alone after you left me. It is a cake of sifted flour and eggs and citron and raisins, *and I love cake*. But now," the boy's voice quavered, "I would not enjoy it if I ate it in a solitary fashion; it would choke me! Sir, I desire to give the cake to you as my gift. Perhaps you will munch it later, when the chill of early morn has set in and you are on the road."

The man did not speak, but his eyes were like stars —instead of candles—as he watched his small host lift the cake from the basket and display its rich goodness. It was only when the boy extended it toward him that he broke into speech.

"Ah, my lad," he said, "you have sustained me with your bread, and we have drunk deep of the same cup. So now we will share this cake, which shall be, through your bounty, my birthday cake. We will apportion it evenly and deftly, and we will eat of it together—you and I. And then you shall wait for the dawn, and I will be on my way. But as I walk along the road I shall see a little lad's face, and shall hear a little lad's voice, and shall remember a little lad's generosity."

Gravely—as if he were handling something infinitely precious—the man took the rich cake into his fingers. Carefully he divided it so that the two sections were equal. He said, "Bless unto us this food, my Father," and the boy was startled, because there was no one else upon the hillside. Then he said,

"This is the cake of life, lad. Enjoy it to the last crumb!"

So he and the boy ate the cake together, and the boy thought that he had never tasted such fare. It was as if the cake's richness were verily the richness of life! As he licked the last crumbs from his fingers he felt that he was gathering force and vigor and purpose. In his

mind's eye, for no reason at all, he saw a picture of himself—robust and handsome and brave—striding down
the road with his weakness cast from him and his chin
high.

"It's like a vision!" he said, but when the man
queried,

"What do you mean, lad?" he hung his head and
was unable to answer.

Indeed, he was silent so long that the man's hand
came to rest lightly upon his shoulder—lightly, but, oh,
so firmly! There was something in the touch that made
tears hang on the boy's lashes, that wrung from him
quick words.

"Oh," he cried, "do not leave me, sir! We could be
such friends, you and I. Come with me to my home and
dwell with my family. My mother will bake many cakes
for you, and my father will share with you of his plenty.
And I—you may have my bed, and my waxed flowers,
and even this fringed shawl that I wear. Do not journey
on, sir! Stay with me, here in Bethlehem."

The man spoke. His voice was like a great bell toll-
ing over hill and valley. "I must go on," he said. "I must
be about my father's business—I must travel toward my
destiny. But I shall never leave you, my lad, for all that.
Lo, I am with you always—even unto the end of the
world!"

Bowing his head in his hands, covering his misted
eyes, the boy was aware of the man's firm fingers traveling up from his shoulder until they touched his hair.
But now he couldn't speak, for a pulse drummed in his

throat, and a strange rhythm was hammering in his ears. When he raised his head, finally, the man was gone, and the hillside was empty—save for the shadows that were the sheep.

The boy sobbed once, and sharply, with a sense of loss. He struggled to his feet. Only he didn't have to struggle, really, for there was a curious lightness about his body, and a feeling of freshness and peace—a peace that transcended the pain of parting. But it was not until he drew the fringed lamb's-wool shawl tighter across his back that he realized how straight he was standing—*and how straight he would always stand.*

The Stranger Child

A Legend

Count Franz Pocci (Translated)

There once lived a laborer who earned his daily bread by cutting wood. His wife and two children, a boy and girl, helped him with his work. The boy's name was Valentine, and the girl's, Marie. They were obedient and pious and the joy and comfort of their poor parents.

One winter evening, this good family gathered about the table to eat their small loaf of bread, while the father read aloud from the Bible. Just as they sat down there came a knock on the window, and a sweet voice called:

"O let me in! I am a little child, and I have nothing to eat, and no place to sleep in. I am so cold and hungry! Please, good people, let me in!"

Valentine and Marie sprang from the table and ran to open the door, saying:

"Come in, poor child, we have but very little ourselves, not much more than thou hast, but what we have we will share with thee."

The stranger Child entered, and going to the fire began to warm his cold hands.

The children gave him a portion of their bread, and said:

"Thou must be very tired; come, lie down in our bed, and we will sleep on the bench here before the fire."

Then answered the stranger Child: "May God in Heaven reward you for your kindness."

They led the little guest to their small room, laid him in their bed, and covered him closely, thinking to themselves:

"Oh, how much we have to be thankful for! We have our nice warm room and comfortable bed, while this Child has nothing but the sky for a roof, and the earth for a couch."

When the parents went to their bed, Valentine and Marie lay down on the bench before the fire, and said one to the other:

"The stranger Child is happy now, because he is so warm! Good night!"

Then they fell asleep.

They had not slept many hours, when little Marie

awoke, and touching her brother lightly, whispered:

"Valentine, Valentine, wake up! Wake up! Listen to the beautiful music at the window."

Valentine rubbed his eyes and listened. He heard the most wonderful singing and the sweet notes of many harps.

> "Blessed Child,
> Thee we greet,
> With sound of harp
> And singing sweet.

> "Sleep in peace,
> Child so bright,
> We have watched thee
> All the night.

[55]

"Blest the home
That holdeth Thee,
Peace, and love,
Its guardians be."

The children listened to the beautiful singing, and it seemed to fill them with unspeakable happiness. Then creeping to the window they looked out.

They saw a rosy light in the east, and, before the house in the snow, stood a number of little children holding golden harps and lutes in their hands, and dressed in sparkling, silver robes.

Full of wonder at this sight, Valentine and Marie continued to gaze out at the window, when they heard a sound behind them, and turning saw the stranger Child standing near. He was clad in a golden garment, and wore a glistening, golden crown upon his soft hair. Sweetly he spoke to the children:

"I am the Christ Child, who wanders about the world seeking to bring joy and good things to loving children. Because you have lodged me this night I will leave with you my blessing."

As the Christ Child spoke He stepped from the door, and breaking off a bough from a fir tree that grew near, planted it in the ground, saying:

"This bough shall grow into a tree, and every year it shall bear Christmas fruit for you."

Having said this He vanished from their sight, together with the silver-clad, singing children—the angels.

And, as Valentine and Marie looked on in wonder,

the fir bough grew, and grew, and grew, into a stately Christmas Tree laden with golden apples, silver nuts, and lovely toys. And after that, every year at Christmas time, the Tree bore the same wonderful fruit.

And you, dear boys and girls, when you gather around your richly decorated trees, think of the two poor children who shared their bread with a stranger child, and be thankful.

O Little Town of Bethlehem

Phillips Brooks

O little town of Bethlehem,
How still we see thee lie;
Above thy deep and dreamless sleep
The silent stars go by;
Yet in thy dark streets shineth
The everlasting light;
The hopes and fears of all the years
Are met in thee tonight.

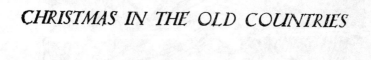

CHRISTMAS IN THE OLD COUNTRIES

Yuletide Customs in Many Lands

Lou Crandall

Christmas in May? It sounds strange, doesn't it? And yet in the early centuries of Christianity, the birthday of Jesus probably was sometimes celebrated in May, sometimes in other months; certainly it was often observed in January. This was because the exact date of the birth of Christ has never been known.

It was in the fourth century that December twenty-fifth was named by Church authorities as the date of the Nativity. And during the next hundred years the celebration of this event on the day we now call Christmas became a custom generally accepted throughout the Christian world. The reason why December twenty-fifth was selected is another mystery. Possibly it was because that was the time when the winter solstice was celebrated in ancient Rome. At any rate, the choice of the twenty-fifth day of December accounts for many of our Christmas customs, for it fell within the time of the big winter festivals and feasts, not only of Rome but also of the pagans in the north.

And now let us see how today, and in other countries than our own, Christmas time is observed.

England is a country where the celebration is a great deal like ours. Christmas Eve the tree is decorated, and stockings are hung in anticipation of a visit from Santa Claus or Father Christmas. Perhaps during the evening a group of singers called "waits" will serenade the household. On Christmas Day there will be gifts and church and a tremendous noontime dinner with roast beef, or goose, and plum pudding.

Possibly the most-loved custom of an English Christmas is that of burning the Yule log—an immense block of wood that fills the fireplace. The Yule log is one of the Christmas customs that has come to us from pagan times when the druids kept sacred fires burning. In the Middle Ages the log was very large. It was carefully chosen long beforehand and it was dragged into the great hall in the midst of much celebration. It was the custom, too, to light the log with a piece of the one left over from the year before.

Now let's travel farther north and see what is going on in two of the Scandinavian countries. Swedish children have their gifts and tree on Christmas Eve, and the big Christmas dinner is that night also. Sometimes exciting gifts are thrown in the front doors by mysterious donors who run away before anyone can find out who they are. Christmas Day itself, the whole family rises extremely early and goes to church.

In Norway also there is a Christmas tree and a grand feast. The gifts are often hidden away in different parts of the house for the children to find. In both of these northern countries sheaves of grain are put on top of the houses or barns or are hung on poles in the yards, that the birds, too, may enjoy a Christmas dinner.

The great gift of Germany to the customs of Christmas is the decorated tree—for many years the heart of German Christmas celebrations. Probably in early times, pagans honored trees during some of their festivities, but it is likely they were not used in connection with Christmas until the sixteenth century. It was Martin Luther, so many people believe, who thought of decorating the first Christmas tree, inspired by watching the beauty of brilliant stars against a dark sky one Christmas Eve.

In Holland and Belgium, Christmas time itself is celebrated mostly by church services. But there is another day the children love; this is the sixth of December, the feast day of St. Nicholas. It is said that during the evening of December fifth, St. Nicholas, dressed in magnificent robes, comes riding on a horse, and goes about inquiring as to the behavior of the children. If the report is satisfactory, in the morning they will find their shoes full of gifts; but if the children are naughty, they are liable to find instead rods of birch!

In France, for grownups, the day of feasting and

visiting is New Year's. Christmas is for the most part a church celebration. But the children are not forgotten at *Noël,* or Christmas time. Christmas Eve they leave their shoes by the chimney, and in the morning they find them full of presents, which they believe have been left for them by the Christ Child, *le petit Jésus.* The end of the Christmas season also brings excitement in the form of a special Twelfth Night cake within which has been baked some little token such as a bean or china figure. Whoever gets the piece of cake containing the token becomes "king" or "queen" for the rest of the party.

As we travel farther south to Italy, we find that here, too, Christmas is mostly a religious occasion. For twenty-four hours before Christmas Eve a strict fast is kept. Then on Christmas Eve a splendid banquet is held, and after it comes the exciting drawing of presents from the Urn of Fate. The Urn is a big crock filled with gifts. These are drawn out, and as sometimes the presents are blanks, there is much excitement and occasionally disappointment among the children. But eventually there is a gift for everyone, so all are happy. Now come the Christmas Eve services in the church. As the families go through the crowded streets, they find them very gay. The streets are bright with bonfires and fireworks, and some of the people are carrying torches.

On Epiphany, which comes on the sixth of January, the Italian children have another treat in store for them. On the Eve of Epiphany, or Twelfth Night, the children hang up their stockings and during the night a little old lady, *Befana,* is believed to come and leave delightful gifts in the stockings of the good children, but only birch rods or charcoal ashes in those of the bad.

Wouldn't it seem strange to celebrate Christmas in the summertime? And yet that is exactly what happens in Australia, where December twenty-fifth occurs during their summer. So, strangely enough, a picnic is often an important part of Christmas Day festivities there.

All the unusual Christmas observances are not in faraway lands, by any means. Right here on our own continent, in Mexico, Christmas is celebrated with a number of interesting customs. Possibly the one the children enjoy most is the breaking of the *pinata*. A *pinata* is a bowl, gaily decorated and filled with little toys and candies and hung up above the heads of the children. The children in turn are blindfolded and given a stick; each has a chance to break the *pinata*. This is not easy to do when one is blindfolded, and many fail. But at last one child will break it—and then what fun!—for everyone rushes to gather up some of the goodies and toys.

In Mexico the gift day for children is not Christmas, but Epiphany. The night before the children place their shoes in the window or at the foot of their beds. Then the next morning, there the shoes are, brimful of presents—gifts, they say, from the Magi on their way to see the Christ Child.

Christmas Pantomime†

A Story of New England

Hugh Walpole

Several weeks before Christmas there appeared upon the town walls and hoardings the pictured announcements of the approaching visit to Polchester of Denny's Great Christmas Pantomine "Dick Whittington." * * *

Just above Martin's the pastry-cook's (where they sold lemon biscuits), near the Cathedral, there was a big wooden hoarding, and on to this was pasted a marvelous representation of Dick and his Cat dining with the King of the Zanzibar Islands. * * * There was another wonderful picture of Dick asleep at the Cross Roads, fairies

† Asterisks show where parts of the original story have been omitted.

watching over him, and London Town in a lighted purple distance—and another of the streets of Old London
with a comic fat serving man, diamond-paned windows,
cobblestones and high pointing eaves to the houses.

Jeremy saw these pictures for the first time during
one of his afternoon walks, and returned home in such
a state of choking excitement that he could not drink his
tea. ˳ ˳ ˳

"We'll all go," said Mr. Cole, in his genial, pastoral
fashion. "Good for us . . . good for us . . . to see the
little ones laugh . . . good for us all."

Only Uncle Samuel said "that nothing would in-
duce him——"

II

I pass swiftly over Christmas Eve, Christmas Day,
and the day after, although I should like to linger upon
these sumptuous dates. Jeremy had a sumptuous time;
Hamlet had a sumptuous time (a whole sugar rat, plates
and plates of bones, and a shoe of Aunt Amy's); Mary
and Helen had sumptuous times in their own feminine
fashion.

Upon the evening of Christmas Eve, when the earth
was snow-lit, and the street lamps sparkled with crystals,
and the rime on the doorsteps crackled beneath one's
feet, Jeremy accompanied his mother on a present-leav-
ing expedition. ˳ ˳ ˳

There followed the Stocking, the Waits, the Carols,
the Turkey, the Christmas Cake, the *Tree,* the Presents,
Snapdragon, Bed. . . . ˳ ˳ ˳ Christmas was over.

From that moment of the passing of Boxing Day it was simply the counting of the minutes to "Dick Whittington." Six days from Boxing Day. . . .

The Day Before The Day arrived, the evening before The Day, the last supper before The Day, the last bed before The Day. . . . Suddenly, like a Jack-in-the-Box, The Day itself.

Then the awful thing happened.

Jeremy awoke to the consciousness that something terrific was about to occur. . . . He dressed with immense speed, as though that would hasten the coming of the evening. He ran into the nursery, carrying the black tie that went under his sailor-collar.

He held it out to the Jampot, who eyed him with disfavor. . . .

"Nurse. Please. Fasten it," he said impatiently.

"And that's not the way to speak, Master Jeremy, and well you know it," she said. " 'Ave you cleaned your teeth?"

"Yes," he answered without hesitation. It was not until the word was spoken that he realized that he had not. . . .

He would have taken the word back, he wanted to take it back—but something held him as though one stronger than he had placed his hand over his mouth. His face flamed.

"You've truly cleaned them?" she said.

"Yes, truly," he answered, his eyes on the ground. Never was there a more obvious liar in all the world.

She said no more; he moved to the fireplace. • • •

After all, he *would* clean them so soon as she went to brush Helen's hair. In a moment what he had said would be true.

But he was miserable. . . . He watched, from under his eyelids, the Jampot. In a moment she must go into Helen's room. But she did not. She stayed for a little arranging the things on the breakfast-table—then suddenly, without a word, she turned into Jeremy's bedchamber. His heart began to hammer. There was an awful pause. . . .

Then, like Judgment, the Jampot appeared again. She stood in the doorway, looking across at him.

"You 'ave *not* cleaned your teeth, Master Jeremy," she said. "The glass isn't touched, nor your toothbrush. . . . You wicked, wicked boy. So it's a liar you've become, added on to all your other wickedness."

"I forgot," he muttered sullenly. "I thought I had."

She smiled the smile of approaching triumph.

"No, you did not," she said. "You knew you'd told a lie. It was in your face. * * * If you think I'm going to let this pass you're making a mighty mistake." . . .

"I don't care what you do," Jeremy shouted. "You can tell anyone you like. I don't care what you do. You're a beastly woman."

She turned upon him, her face purple. "That's enough, Master Jeremy," she said, her voice low and trembling. * * * "You'll be sorry for this before you're much older. . . . You see."

There was then an awful and sickly pause. Jeremy seemed to himself to be sinking lower and lower into a damp clammy depth of degradation. * * *

His feelings were utterly confused. He supposed that he was terribly wicked. But he did not feel wicked. He only felt miserable, sick and defiant. Mary and Helen came in, their eyes open to a crisis. * * *

Then Mr. Cole came in as was his daily habit—for a moment before his breakfast.

"Well, here are you all," he cried. "Ready for to-night? No breakfast yet? Why, now . . . ?"

Then perceiving, as all practiced fathers instantly must, that the atmosphere was sinful, he changed his voice to that of the Children's Sunday Afternoon Service—a voice well known in his family.

"Please, sir," began the Jampot, "I'm sorry to 'ave to tell you, sir, that Master Jeremy's not been at all good this morning."

"Well, Jeremy," he said, turning to his son, "what is it?"

Jeremy's face, raised to his father's, was hard and set and sullen.

"I've told a lie," he said; "I said I'd cleaned my teeth when I hadn't. Nurse went and looked, and then I called her a beastly woman."

The Jampot's face expressed a grieved and at the same time triumphant confirmation of this.

"You told a lie?" Mr. Cole's voice was full of a lingering sorrow.

"Yes," said Jeremy.

"Are you sorry?"

"I'm sorry that I told a lie, but I'm not sorry I called Nurse a beastly woman "

"Jeremy!"

"No, I'm not. She *is* a beastly woman."

Mr. Cole was always at a loss when anyone defied him, even though it were only a small boy of eight. He took refuge now in his ecclesiastical and parental authority.

"I'm very distressed—very distressed indeed. I hope that punishment, Jeremy, will show you how wrong you have been. I'm afraid you cannot come with us to the Pantomime tonight."

At that judgment a quiver for an instant held Jeremy's face, turning it, for that moment, into something shapeless and old. His heart had given a wild leap of terror and dismay. ✻ ✻ ✻

"And until you've apologized to Nurse for your rudeness you must remain by yourself. I shall forbid your sisters to speak to you. Mary and Helen, you are not to speak to your brother until he has apologized to Nurse."

"Yes, Father," said Helen.

"Oh, Father, mayn't he come tonight?" said Mary.

"No, Mary, I'm afraid not."

A tear rolled down her cheek. "It won't be any fun without Jeremy," she said. * * *

The day dragged its weary length along, and Jeremy scarcely moved from his corner by the fire. * * *

The evening came on; the curtains were drawn. Tea arrived; still Jeremy sat there, not speaking, not raising his eyes, a condemned creature. * * *

The girls went to dress. Seven o'clock struck. They were taken downstairs by Nurse, who had her evening out. Rose, the housemaid, would sit with Master Jeremy.

Doors closed, doors opened, voices echoed, carriage wheels were heard.

Jeremy and Hamlet were left to themselves. . . .

III

The last door had closed, and the sudden sense that everyone had gone and that he might behave now as he pleased, removed the armor in which all day he had encased himself.

He raised his head, looked about the deserted nursery, and then, with the sudden consciousness of that other lighted and busied place where Whittington was pursuing his adventures, he burst into tears. * * *

He did not even now feel really wicked, but he saw quite clearly that there was one world for liars and one for truthful men. He wanted, terribly badly, someone to tell him that he was still in the right world. . . . . . .

Then the door suddenly opened, and in came Uncle Samuel.

Jeremy had forgotten his uncle, and now blinked up at him from the floor, where he was squatting, rather ashamed of his swollen eyes and red nose.

Uncle Samuel, however, had no time for details; he was apparently in a hurry. . . .

"Come on," he said, "or we shall be too late."

Jeremy choked. "Too late?" he repeated.

"You're coming, aren't you—to the Pantomime? They sent me back for you." . . .

"I—don't—understand," Jeremy stammered.

"Well, if you don't understand in half a shake," said Uncle Samuel, "you won't see any of the show at all. Go on. Wash your face. There are streaks of dirt all down it as though you were a painted Indian; stick on your cap and coat and boots and come along."

Exactly as one moves in sleep so Jeremy now moved. . . . He found his boots and cap and coat and then, deliberately keeping from him the thought of the Pantomime lest he should suddenly wake up, he said:

"I'm ready, Uncle. . . . Is it really true? Are we going—really?"

"Of course we're going. Come on—step out or you'll miss the Giant."

"But—but—oh!" he drew a deep breath. "Then they don't think me a liar any more?"

"They—who?"

"Father and Mother and everyone."

"Don't you think about them. You'd better enjoy yourself."

"But you said you wouldn't go to the Pantomime—not for anything?"

"Well, I've changed my mind. Don't talk so much. You know I hate you children chattering. Always got something to say."

So Jeremy was silent. They raced down Orange Street, Jeremy being almost carried off his feet. This was exactly like a dream. This rushing movement and the way that the lampposts ran up to you as though they were going to knock you down, and the way that the stars crackled and sputtered and trembled overhead. But Uncle Samuel's hand was flesh and blood, and the heel of Jeremy's right shoe hurt him and he felt the tickle of his sailor-collar at the back of his neck, just as he did when he was awake.

Then there they were at the Assembly Rooms door, Jeremy having become so breathless that Uncle Samuel had to hold him up for a moment or he'd have fallen.

"Bit too fast for you, was it? Well, you shouldn't be so fat. You eat too much. Now we're not going to sit with your father and mother—there isn't room for you there. So don't you go calling out to them or anything. We're sitting in the back and you'd better be quiet or they'll turn you out."

"I'll be quiet," gasped Jeremy.

Uncle Samuel paused at a lighted hole in the wall

and spoke to a large lady in black silk who was drinking a cup of tea. Jeremy caught the jingle of money. Then they moved forward, stumbling in the dark up a number of stone steps, pushing at a heavy black curtain, then suddenly bathed in a bewildering glow of light and scent and color.

Jeremy's first impression, as he fell into this new world, was of an ugly, harsh, but funny voice crying out very loudly indeed: "Oh, my great aunt! Oh, my great aunt! Oh, my great aunt!" A roar of laughter rose about him, almost lifting him off his feet.   * * *

He was aware then of a strong smell of oranges, of Uncle Samuel pushing him forward, of stumbling over boots, knees, and large hands that were clapping in his very nose, of falling into a seat and then clinging to it as though it was his only hope in this strange puzzling world. The high funny voice rose again: "Oh, my great aunt! Oh, my great aunt!" And again it was followed by the rough roar of delighted laughter.

He was aware then that about him on every side gas was sizzling, and then, as he recovered slowly his breath, his gaze was drawn to the great blaze of light in the distance, against which figures were dimly moving, and from the heart of which the strange voice came. * * *

He saw that it was a shop—and he loved shops. His heart beat thickly as his eyes traveled up and up and up over the rows and rows of shelves; here were bales of cloth, red and green and blue; carpets from the East, table covers, sheets and blankets. Behind the long yellow counters young men in strange clothes were standing. In the middle of the scene was a funny old woman, her hat tumbling off her head, her shabby skirt dragging, large boots, and a red nose. It was from this strange creature that the deep ugly voice proceeded. She had, this old woman, a number of bales of cloth under her arms, and she tried to carry them all, but one slipped, and then another, and then another; she bent to pick them up and her hat fell off; she turned for her hat and all the bales tumbled together. Jeremy began to laugh—everyone laughed. . . .

As a finale to the first half of the entertainment there was given Dick's dream at the Cross Roads. He lay on the hard ground, his head upon his bundle, the cat as large as he watching sympathetically beside him. In the distance were the lights of London, and then, out of the half dusk, fairies glittering with stars and silver danced up and down the dusky road whilst all the London bells rang out "Turn again, Whittington, Lord Mayor of London." . . .

When the gas rose once again, sizzling like crackling bacon, Jeremy was white with excitement. . . . The huge lady in the seat next to Jeremy almost swallowed him up, so that he peered out from under her thick arm, and heard every crunch and crackle of the peppermints that she was enjoying. He grew hotter and hotter. . . . But he did not mind. Discomfort only emphasized his happiness. Then, peering forward beneath that stout black arm, he suddenly perceived, far below in the swimming distance, the back of his mother, the tops of the heads of Mary and Helen, the stiff white collar of his father, and the well-known coral necklace of Aunt Amy. . . .

"Shall I wave to them?" he asked excitedly of Uncle Samuel.

"No, no," said his uncle very hurriedly. "Nonsense. They wouldn't see you if you did. Leave them alone."

He felt immensely superior to them up where he was, and he wouldn't have changed places with them for anything. He gave a little sigh of satisfaction. "I could drop an orange on to Aunt Amy's head," he said. "Wouldn't she jump!"

"You must keep quiet," said Uncle Samuel. "You're good enough as you are."

"I'd rather be here," said Jeremy. "It's beautifully hot here and there's a *lovely* smell."

"There is," said Uncle Samuel.

Then the gas went down, and the curtain went up, and Dick, now in a suit of red silk with golden buttons, continued his adventures. I have not space here to describe in detail the further events of his life—how, receiving a telegram from the King of the Zanzibars about the plague of rats, he took ship with his cat and Alderman Fitzwarren and his wife, how they were all swallowed by a whale, cast up by a most lucky chance on the Zanzibars, nearly cooked by the natives, and rescued by the King of the Zanzibars' beautiful daughter, killed all the rats, were given a huge feast, with dance and song, and how Dick, although tempted by the dusky Princess, refused a large fortune and returned to Alice of Eastcheap, the true lady of his heart. * * * And then there was a Transformation Scene, in which roses turned into tulips and tulips into the Hall of Gold, down whose blazing steps marched stout representatives of all the nations.

It was in the middle of this last thrilling spectacle, when Jeremy's heart was in his mouth and he was so deeply excited that he did not know whether it were he or the lady next to him who was eating peppermints, that his uncle plucked him by the sleeve and said in his ear: "Come on. It's close on the end. We must go."

Jeremy very reluctantly got up, and stumbled out over knees and legs. * * *

He was dragged through the black curtain, down the stone steps, and into the street.

"But it wasn't the end," he said.

"It will be in one minute," said his uncle. "And I want us to get home first."

"Why?" said Jeremy.

"Never you mind. Come on; we'll race it."

They arrived home breathless, and then, once again in the old familiar hall, Uncle Samuel said:

"Now you nip up to the nursery, and then they'll never know you've been out at all."

"Never know?" said Jeremy. "But you said they'd sent for me."

"Well," said Uncle Samuel, "that wasn't exactly true. As a matter of fact, they don't know you were there."

"Oh!" said Jeremy, the corner of his mouth turning down. "Then I've told a lie again!"

"Nonsense!" said Uncle Samuel impatiently. "It wasn't you; it was I."

"And doesn't it matter your telling lies?" asked Jeremy.

The answer to this difficult question was, happily for Uncle Samuel, interrupted by the arrival of the household, who had careened up Orange Street in a cab.

When Mr. and Mrs. Cole saw Jeremy standing in the hall, his greatcoat still on and his muffler round his neck, there was a fine scene of wonder and amazement.

Uncle Samuel explained. "It was my fault. I told him you'd forgiven him and sent for him to come, after all. He's in an awful state now that you shouldn't forgive him."

Whatever they thought of Uncle Samuel, this was

obviously neither the time nor the place to speak out. Mrs. Cole looked at her son. His body defiant, sleepy, excited. His mouth was obstinate, but his eyes appealed to her on the scene of the common marvelous experience that they had just enjoyed.

She hugged him.

"And you won't tell a lie again, will you, Jeremy, dear?"

"Oh, no!" And then, hurrying on: "And when the old woman tumbled down the steps, Mother, wasn't it lovely? And the fairies in Dick Whittington's sleep, and when the furniture all fell all over the place——"

He went slowly upstairs to the nursery, the happiest boy in the kingdom. But through all his happiness there was this puzzle: Uncle Samuel had told a lie, and no one had thought that it mattered. There were good lies and bad ones then. Or was it that grown-up people could tell lies and children mustn't? . . .

He tumbled into the warm, lighted nursery half asleep. There was Hamlet watching in front of the Jampot's sewing machine.

He would have things to think about for years and years and years. . . .

There was the Jampot.

"I'm sorry I called you a beastly woman," he said. * * *

Christmas Sheaves

A Story of Norway

Nora Burglon

INGRID AND SVERRE, IN FAR-OFF NORWAY, DID
NOT EXPECT TO BE REMEMBERED BY THE CHRIST-
MAS NISSE, AND IF THEY HAD FORGOTTEN THEIR
DUTY TO THE BIRDS . . .

Hardanger fiord wound its silent course in and out
between the mountain walls. Here and there along the
strand rose gray wisps of smoke from the cottages where
the housewives had already begun the Christmas baking.

It was Saint Lucia Day, the thirteenth of December, so of course baking had been done long before this
day, although that could not exactly be called the Yule

baking, for it was best to have plenty of good food to eat in the house on Lucia Day* if one expected abundance through the year to come.

To Sverre and Ingrid it was a very wonderful day because it was the last of school for the year. Still, it was not for that reason that the two little croft in Lovdalen were glad to have it come. It was because of what might hang upon the spruce tree in the corner of the old log schoolhouse.

"I'm not expecting anything," announced Sverre, a little bitterly. "There wasn't anything last year."

"Yes, but that was last year," said Ingrid, "perhaps the Christmas Nisse† is richer this year than last."

The children of the rich were always looked to first by even the Yule Nisse and the crofter‡ children had to wait to the last. If there was anything left, they got it. If there was not, they went without, just the same as in everything else . . .

The schoolroom was all abustle when Ingrid and Sverre came in. Everyone was wearing his best clothes today. The boys wore their fine "vadmal" suits—all blue —with the blue caps. The brass buttons upon their coats were burnished until they shone like the sun, and the red

* Saint Lucia Day—This is the day of celebration given over to the consummation of the harvest, an old Viking custom celebrated in Scandinavia for five thousand years, originating in the worship of Odin brought to Scandinavia by the Asa folk (the Asiatics). Lucia goes back to Asiatic Lucina, goddess of the harvest, light and life, also Diana. For this reason the thirteenth of December ushers in the Yule season.

† Nisse—It is thought that the Christmas elf, the Nisse (pronounced "nĭs"), brings the Yule gifts in Norway.

‡ Crofter—One who lives on a small rented farm, called a croft.

pompons on the ends of the garter bands bobbed about from side to side as if they were afraid they would not see and hear everything that was to happen this day.

The girls wore their blue, twin-cornered caps with the binding of bright homespun ribbons. They wore their fine Hardanger aprons which were embroidered until they looked as if made up of snowflakes. Everyone wore silver buckles and ornaments and some of the bodices were so bright they made one's eyes blink when one looked at them. But who cared about what anyone wore? The children were all thinking about exactly the same thing. They were wondering what they were going to get off the Christmas tree.

"I know what I am going to get," said Ulf, "I am going to get a five-bladed knife with my initials on it."

"Huh, how do you know that?" said Sverre, for he was wondering how Ulf, who never got his lessons, was going to get anything so wonderful from the Yule Nisse.

"I know because that is what I want," said Ulf, "and I get whatever I want."

"Why don't you get a perfect spelling lesson, then?" said Ingrid.

"Yes, why don't you?" Sverre pointed out, for who did not know what a sort of a one Ulf was? He had to stand in the shame-corner every solitary day. But it was just exactly as Ulf had said. He got the five-bladed knife and it even had his initials upon it, and the initials were in silver and burnished like the buttons on Ulf's jacket.

"See, what did I tell you?" he whispered over to Sverre. Both Ingrid and Sverre sat there and watched now. Gifts went out in every direction but not a one came their way. Could it be that the Yule Nisse could have the heart to give to such a careless one as Ulf and yet pass them by? The boys and girls were now eating their sugar plums and their nuts, while the two crofter children sat there in their seats and tried to make themselves as small as they could.

"That is all," said the schoolmaster. The gifts had been given out, now, and the children were dismissed.

"Ingrid and Sverre got nothing at all," said the children, when they gathered outside to examine the gifts. They said that as if they rather thought the two of them could not have been any too good or the Nisse would surely not have treated them so badly.

Ingrid looked at her brother. His face was buried in his scarf so that there was nothing showing between the cap and the coat but his nose. She knew that he was trying to hide within himself so that the rest of the children would not see that there were tears in his eyes. Ingrid forgot, now, that there had been tears in her own eyes but a moment before. She took up her ski staff and set out after her brother. "Sverre," she said, "the rest of them act just as if we were going to get nothing at all for Christmas."

"Well, we aren't, either," said Sverre. "We're not going to get a single thing."

"How you talk," she answered. "Why, can't you see that the Nisse is doing this just to see how we are going to act? If we act as if what he had done was exactly as it should be, then we, too, will get something nice."

Sverre wiped his tears and gave a heavy sigh. Suddenly it was as if he saw a ray of hope again. Perhaps it was as his sister had said. So the two of them walked on upon their skis in silence until they came home to the little croft. A flock of snowbirds flew down upon the snow inside of the gate as they did every evening. They were waiting for the crumbs the children saved for them out of their lunch. Out the crumbs went upon the snow while the children stood by and watched the birds pick them up. Suddenly Sverre grasped his sister by the arm and said, "Ingrid, do you know what?"

"What?"

"We haven't got a sheaf* of grain for our birds this year."

To the minds of both of them now came the thought that perhaps these birds were looking forward to their Christmas gift just as the two of them had looked for a gift at school. Should it be said of them that they had not even enough for the birds?

"No," said Sverre, "we must get some grain so that our birds shall not be without their Christmas dinner." Indeed, it was only the stingiest of people who did not put out a Christmas dinner for the cats and dogs who had no home, and the poor birds who had to fly from branch to branch in search of something to eat and a place where they might warm their feet. True, the crofter folks sometimes had only a crust of dry bread to put out for their birds, but it was something, anyway. However, this year the birds at Lovdalen were to have their sheaf as they had all other years. Had it not been that the harvest was so poor that year, there would have been a sheaf or two set away at threshing time, but the mistress of Lovdalen had needed every kernel to make bread.

*　　*　　*　　*　　*

"Well, what are we to do to earn money enough to buy a bundle of grain?" demanded Ingrid.

"We might get a couple of fir trees out of the woods

* Sheaf—Putting a sheaf of grain out for the birds is a Norwegian custom from early Christian times. Even today the Scandinavians feel a kinship with all nature and its creatures at the Christmas season. In olden times all creatures were considered brothers at Yule.

and take them to town. Perhaps someone would buy them from us."

Sverre always talked all matters over with his sister in this way before he was exactly certain about anything. "Yes, you are right, Sverre," she said, "that is the very thing to do."

So the next day Sverre and his sister went to the forest and chopped down two fir trees.

When the trees were down, the two of them set out with a tree apiece dragging after them on the end of a cord. In Rosendal almost everyone had set up his two trees outside of the doorpost. "It looks as if the folks here in the city are commencing to celebrate Christmas already," said Sverre. "Supposing everyone has bought a tree already?"

"Oh, no," said Ingrid, "surely someone in this large city has not had time to get a tree yet." So the two of them went from house to house and rapped at every door but nobody seemed to want those two Christmas trees which had come to the city behind the skis of the two from Lovdalen. "We have our trees standing in the back yard," the housewives would say, "there has not been time to put them up yet." With that the doors would go shut and the two would move on to the next house . . .

Night came at last and the two were still going from house to house. Tired they were and discouraged, yet the long road home lay before them, and the Christmas trees were still unsold.

At last Ingrid said, "I suppose we might as well go home, for it is becoming so dark Mother will worry about us if we stay much longer."

Sverre nodded. "Let us go around by the place where they sell the sheaves," he said. "It is going to seem good to look at a sheaf even if we have not enough to buy one." So together they went over to the store, with the poor trees still dragging after them in the snow.

The sheaves were hung about the inside of a booth there, and it looked exactly like harvest time around the man who was selling them.

There they stood, the two of them, and looked at the golden sheaves which seemed to be reaching out toward them.

"Can I sell you a couple?" invited the man.

"No," said Sverre, for he was the boy and should do the talking, of course. "We haven't sold our trees yet."

"Have you tried at the houses?"

"We have gone to every place in town," replied the boy, "but it looks as if our birds will have to go without their Christmas dinner this year."

"Oh, it is like that," said the man. "Well, you have not asked me yet, and I have no trees at all."

"Would you buy our trees?" cried the two of them together. "Would you?"

"I'll trade with you," offered the man. "I'll give you a couple of bundles for your trees." So the trade was made and now it was the bundles that went home on the end of the string.

"It is dark," said Sverre, "and that is a very good thing, for now the birds will not see what we are going to give them for Christmas." So the two golden bundles were stored away in the goat house until Christmas.

One could just never believe that time could creep by so slowly. In fact, it rather looked as if Christmas Eve was never coming at all, but come it did just the same, and as soon as dark had fallen the two of them crept out together and fastened a sheaf on each of the gateposts. What a surprise that was going to be for the birds in the morning! Perhaps they would think that the Yule Nisse had brought it for them.

It was really remarkable how funny those sheaf-crowned gateposts looked in the night, almost like two people standing there bowing and nodding to each other.

* * * * *

Ulf's grandfather, the stingy old Colonel who lived on the hill and never gave bird or beast a thing, went to the city to buy Ulf some Christmas gifts. He did that every year, just as if the Yule Nisse did not give Ulf enough without having the grandfather give, too. It would have been better to give to the birds who sat beneath his window, or to the crofter people who worked so long and so hard for him.

He had cakes and sugar plums and toys all wrapped up in fine packages which he had put in the back of his sleigh and were going to be given to Ulf on Christmas morning. As he came riding by the croft house his horse saw the two gateposts which appeared to be standing there nodding and bowing to each other. The horse became terrified and gave a leap into the air which almost sent the old Colonel headlong into the snow. Then he shot out over the road as if all the Trolls in Bloxberg were after him. Out flew the packages in the back of the sled and were lodged right against the gate of the croft house, as if someone with a pack on his back had walked up and set them there.

When the frightened horse finally got the Colonel home, the old man went to fetch his packages only to find that there was not a one there. "Somebody has taken my Christmas gifts," stormed the old man and he sputtered and fumed as if there were not plenty of gifts where those had come from and money with which to buy more. Well, it certainly looked as if Ulf was not to get any gifts, so perhaps it was well the Nisse remembered him.

Then suddenly there came a little weak rap upon the door . . .

The gruff old man . . . threw it open, thinking that some beggar perhaps had come to his grand house to beg for a few coppers for Christmas. When he saw two children standing there he said, "Well, what do you two want?"

"We saw when your horse ran away," said Sverre. "Later we found these packages in front of our gate, so we thought you had lost them." With that he set a burlap sack down upon the doorstep and took out every one of the lost packages.

"Well, well," said the old man . . . as he picked them up, "it was very good of you to bring them back to me; I am very sure the Nisse will not forget you for this."

"Oh, the Nisse has other matters to tend to without remembering two such as us," said Sverre; then he wished the old man a happy Yuletide and together the two went down the glistening path back to the road.

"Well," said Ingrid, "it was good to at least get a look into a house where there is so much peace and plenty." But she of course could not know that it was she and her brother who had brought the peace into this grand house.

Early the next morning, as soon as the sun was up, Ingrid and Sverre were out of their beds looking in their stockings to see if the Nisse had brought them anything, but they were as empty as they had been all other mornings.

"On account of the poor harvest this year," said the mother, "the Nisse has had to pass many by this Christmas." But the mother's words were of little comfort to the two children who had found nothing for them either at home or at school. Quickly they slipped into their clothes and crept outside. Both of them felt like crying but they did not want the mother to see that they were such babies they had to cry on Christmas morning.

"Let us go out and see if the birds have found their gift," Ingrid suggested, drying her tears upon the corner of her shawl. Sverre said nothing but followed his sister out to the gate. Long before they got there they could see that there was something outside of the gate, but neither of them dared say, or even hope that it might be something for them. However, when the gate swung open they did see with their own eyes that there really were packages there. "Perhaps the Yule Nisse was in such great hurry he did not have time to bring them inside," they cried and in they flew with their arms full. "Look," they cried, "Mother! Look! The Yule Nisse has brought us something for Christmas."

The mother looked and thought to herself that the packages did not look so different from those which the children had returned last night to the great house upon the hill.

The wrapping and the string came off and who could have thought that even a Nisse could be so wonderful. The whole family had cakes and white bread for breakfast and sugar plums when the meal was over; then there was nothing to do but sit down and play with the toys. Such a grand Christmas there certainly had never been at Lovdalen before, for today even the birds hovered over the gateposts at the croft house like a strange halo over the tops of the sheaves.

The great house on top of the hill seemed to smile almost tenderly upon the little croft house today, but the two children had forgotten that there were any other houses in the valley beside their own. Today that little home contained all that their hearts desired.

Finally Ingrid looked up from her toys and said, "It was as I said. The Nisse was only trying us out to learn what sort of people we are." But Sverre was too busy with his new hammer by the fireplace to remember that the Christmas Nisse had at any time in the past forgotten the two who lived in the humble little croft house at Lovdalen.

CHRISTMAS IN AMERICA

The First New England Christmas

Gertrude L. Stone and M. Grace Fickett

It was a warm and pleasant Saturday—that twenty-third of December, 1620. The winter wind had blown itself away in the storm of the day before, and the air was clear and balmy.

The people on board the *Mayflower* were glad of the pleasant day. It was three long months since they had started from Plymouth, in England, to seek a home across the ocean. Now they had come into a harbor that they named New Plymouth, in the country of New England.

Other people called these voyagers Pilgrims, which means wanderers. A long while before, the Pilgrims had lived in England; later they made their home with the Dutch in Holland; finally they had said good-by to their friends in Holland and in England, and had sailed away to America.

There were only one hundred and two of the Pilgrims on the *Mayflower,* but they were brave and strong and full of hope. Now the *Mayflower* was the only home they had; yet if this weather lasted they might soon have warm log cabins to live in. This very afternoon the men had gone ashore to cut down the large trees.

The women of the *Mayflower* were busy, too. Some were spinning, some knitting, some sewing. It was so bright and pleasant that Mistress Rose Standish had taken her knitting out and had gone to sit a little while on deck. She was too weak to face rough weather, and she wanted to enjoy the warm sunshine and the clear salt air. By her side was Mistress Brewster, the minister's wife. Everybody loved Mistress Standish and Mistress Brewster, for neither of them ever spoke unkindly.

The air on deck would have been warm even on a colder day, for in one corner a bright fire was burning. It would seem strange now would it not, to see a fire on the deck of a vessel? But in those days, when the weather was pleasant, people on shipboard did their cooking on deck.

The Pilgrims had no stoves, and Mistress Carver's maid had built this fire on a large hearth covered with sand. She had hung a great kettle on the crane over the fire, where the onion soup for supper was now simmering slowly.

Near the fire sat a little girl, busily playing and singing to herself. Little Remember Allerton was only six years old, but she liked to be with Hannah, Mistress Carver's maid. This afternoon Remember had been watching Hannah build the fire and make the soup. Now the little girl was playing with the Indian arrowheads her father had brought her the night before. She was singing the words of the old psalm:

"Shout to Jehovah, all the earth,
Serve ye Jehovah with gladness; before
him bow with singing mirth."

"Ah, child, methinks the children of Old England are singing different words from those today," spoke Hannah at length, with a faraway look in her eyes.

"Why, Hannah? What songs are the little English children singing now?" questioned Remember in surprise.

"It lacks but two days of Christmas, child, and in my old home everybody is singing Merry Christmas songs."

"But thou hast not told me what is Christmas!" persisted the child.

"Ah, me! Thou dost not know, 'tis true. Christmas, Remember, is the birthday of the Christ Child, of Jesus, whom thou hast learned to love," Hannah answered softly.

"But what makes the English children so happy then? And we are English, thou hast told me, Hannah. Why don't we keep Christmas, too?"

"In sooth we are English, child. But the reason why we do not sing the Christmas carols or play the Christmas games makes a long, long story, Remember. Hannah cannot tell it so that little children will understand. Thou must ask some other, child."

Hannah and the little girl were just then near the two women on the deck, and Remember said:

"Mistress Brewster, Hannah sayeth she knoweth not how to tell why Love and Wrestling and Constance and the others do not sing the Christmas songs or play the Christmas games. But thou wilt tell me, wilt thou not?" she added coaxingly.

A sad look came into Mistress Brewster's eyes, and Mistress Standish looked grave, too. No one spoke for a few seconds, until Hannah said almost sharply: "Why could we not burn a Yule log Monday, and make some meal into little cakes for the children?"

"Nay, Hannah," answered the gentle voice of Mistress Brewster. "Such are but vain shows and not for those of us who believe in holier things. But," she added, with a kind glance at little Remember, "wouldst thou like to know why we have left Old England and do not keep the Christmas Day? Thou canst not understand it all, child, and yet it may do thee no harm to hear the story. It may help thee to be a brave and happy little girl in the midst of our hard life."

"Surely it can do no harm, Mistress Brewster," spoke Rose Standish, gently. "Remember is a little Pilgrim now, and she ought, methinks, to know something of the reason for our wandering. Come here, child, and

sit by me, while good Mistress Brewster tells thee how cruel men have made us suffer. Then will I sing thee one of the Christmas carols."

With these words she held out her hands to little Remember, who ran quickly to the side of Mistress Standish, and eagerly waited for the story to begin.

"We have not always lived in Holland, Remember. Most of us were born in England, and England is the best country in the world. 'Tis a land to be proud of, Remember, though some of its rulers have been wicked and cruel.

"Long before you were born, when your mother was a little girl, the English king said that everybody in the land ought to think as he thought, and go to a church like his. He said he would send us away from England if we did not do as he ordered. Now, we could not think as he did on holy matters, and it seemed wrong to us to obey him. So we decided to go to a country where we might worship as we pleased."

"What became of that cruel king, Mistress Brewster?"

"He ruleth England now. But thou must not think too hardly of him. He doth not understand, perhaps. Right will win some day, Remember, though there may be bloody war before peace cometh. And I thank God that we, at least, shall not be called on to live in the midst of the strife," she went on, speaking more to herself than to the little girl.

"We decided to go to Holland, out of the reach of the king. We were not sure whether it was best to move or not, but our hearts were set on God's ways. We trusted Him in whom we believed. Yes," she went on, "and shall we not keep on trusting Him?"

And Rose Standish, remembering the little stock of food that was nearly gone, the disease that had come upon many of their number, and the five who had died that month, answered firmly: "Yes. He who has led us thus far will not leave us now."

They were all silent a few seconds. Presently Remember said: "Then did ye go to Holland, Mistress Brewster?"

"Yes," she said. "Our people all went over to Holland, where the Dutch folk live and the little Dutch children clatter about with their wooden shoes. There thou wast born, Remember, and my own children, and there we lived in love and peace.

"And yet, we were not wholly happy. We could not talk well with the Dutch, and so we could not set right what was wrong among them. 'Twas so hard to earn money that many had to go back to England. And worst of all, Remember, we were afraid that you and little Bartholomew and Mary and Love and Wrestling and all the rest would not grow to be good girls and boys. And so we have come to this new country to teach our children to be pure and noble."

After another silence Remember spoke again: "I thank thee, Mistress Brewster. And I will try to be a good girl. But thou didst not tell me about Christmas after all."

"Nay, child, but now I will. There are long services on that day in every church where the king's friends go. But there are parts of these services which we cannot approve; and so we think it best not to follow the other customs that the king's friends observe on Christmas.

"They trim their houses with mistletoe and holly so that everything looks gay and cheerful. Their other name for the Christmas time is the Yuletide, and the big log that is burned then is called the Yule log. The children like to sit around the hearth in front of the great, blazing Yule log, and listen to stories of long, long ago.

"At Christmas there are great feasts in England, too. No one is allowed to go hungry, for the rich people on that day always send meat and cakes to the poor folk round about.

"But we like to make all our days Christmas days,

Remember. We try never to forget God's gifts to us, and they remind us always to be good to other people."

"And the Christmas carols, Mistress Standish? What are they?"

"On Christmas Eve and early on Christmas morning," Rose Standish answered, "little children go about from house to house, singing Christmas songs. 'Tis what I like best in all the Christmas cheer. And I promised to sing thee one, did I not?"

Then Mistress Standish sang in her clear, sweet voice the quaint old English words:

> As Joseph was a-walking,
>   He heard an angel sing:
> "This night shall be the birth-time
>   Of Christ, the heavenly King.
>
> "He neither shall be born
>   In housen nor in hall,
> Nor in the place of Paradise,
>   But in an ox's stall.
>
> "He neither shall be clothèd
>   In purple nor in pall,
> But in the fair white linen
>   That usen babies all.
>
> "He neither shall be rockèd
>   In silver nor in gold,
> But in a wooden manger
>   That resteth in the mould."

As Joseph was a-walking
There did an angel sing,
And Mary's child at midnight
Was born to be our King.

Then be ye glad, good people,
This night of all the year,
And light ye up your candles,
For His star it shineth clear.

Before the song was over, Hannah had come on deck again, and was listening eagerly. "I thank thee, Mistress Standish," she said, the tears filling her blue eyes. " 'Tis long, indeed, since I have heard that song."

"Would it be wrong for me to learn to sing those words, Mistress Standish?" gently questioned the little girl.

"Nay, Remember, I trow not. The song shall be thy Christmas gift."

Then Mistress Standish taught the little girl one verse after another of the sweet old carol, and it was not long before Remember could say it all.

The next day was dull and cold, and on Monday, the twenty-fifth, the sky was still overcast. There was no bright Yule log in the *Mayflower,* and no holly trimmed the little cabin.

The Pilgrims were true to the faith they loved. They held no special services. They made no gifts. Instead, they went again to the work of cutting the trees, and no one murmured at his hard lot.

"We went on shore," one man wrote in his diary,

"some to fell timber, some to saw, some to rive, and some to carry; so no man rested all that day."

As for little Remember, she spent the day on board the *Mayflower*. She heard no one speak of England or sigh for the English home across the sea. But she did not forget Mistress Brewster's story; and more than once that day, as she was playing by herself, she fancied that she was in front of some English home, helping the English children sing their Christmas songs.

And both Mistress Allerton and Mistress Standish, whom God was soon to call away from their earthly home, felt happier and stronger as they heard the little girl singing:

> He neither shall be born
>   In housen nor in hall,
>   Nor in the place of Paradise,
>   But in an ox's stall.

Little Girl of Long Ago

Marjorie Barrows

Little girl of long ago,
    Did you love your Christmas, too?
I like to watch my candles glow,
    And think of you.

Christmas stockings, Christmas toys—
    Santa never brought you one,
But didn't Pilgrim girls and boys
    Have some fun?

When your daily work was through
    And frosty stars shone in the night,
You told stories, didn't you,
    By candlelight?

And roasted apples, popped some corn,
  And then, perhaps, began to sing
A carol for the Baby born
  To be our King?

Christmas carolers draw near,
  Singing now the songs you knew,
And I almost think I hear
  You singing, too. . . .

A Christmas Gift for the General

A Story of the Revolution

Jeannette Covert Nolan

Kennet, at the window, thought that the day was not at all like Christmas. The street he looked into was silent, almost desolate; the few people passing walked quickly with bent heads, as if they were cold, or sad— or both. Their feet left moist black imprints in the banked snow.

Christmas? Kennet sighed, yearning in his heart for other, better years, when peace was abroad in the land and a holiday could be celebrated in proper fashion; when Hessian troops remained across the ocean where they belonged; when the little town of Trenton was not hushed, terrified, but a pleasant place in which to live, to make merry with friends and to share presents and gay greetings. Today Kennet hadn't offered or received a single Christmas present—not one!—and this, to him, seemed tragedy indeed.

He sighed, and Grandfather, hearing the mournful sound, rose from his fireside chair and hobbled over to lay a comforting hand on his shoulder.

"What ails you, lad?"

Ah, but Grandfather knew. Grandfather might be old and so crippled now by rheumatism that he must stay always indoors, crouching over the logs to warm his ancient, aching joints; yet his spirit was youthful, strong. In Grandfather's breast burned the pure flame of patriotism. He gripped Kennet's arm and sighed, too.

"Is it true," Kennet asked, turning, "as they are saying: that General Washington must lose the war?"

The old man pursed withered lips. "Lately all reports have been discouraging. The soldiers suffer from dreadful cold, from lack of food and supplies. A dark hour for our country, very dark. But," Grandfather ended bravely, "there's still hope. Maybe in the spring our luck will change."

"You don't mean the Hessians will be quartered here until *spring!*" Kennet wailed. "Oh, but we couldn't bear it. Those harsh, impudent——"

Grandfather lifted a warning finger. Kennet must not denounce the Hessians, he said. No, they were here, occupying Trenton, taking the best of everything and

living handsomely, while townsfolk skimped, pinched and went hungry. They couldn't be ousted; therefore they must be tolerated—the Hessians, King George's hireling troops.

"Don't grumble," Grandfather advised.

But as he hobbled painfully back to his chair, he muttered under his breath that he would give his own life gladly, poor old thing that it was, if only with it he might aid the cause of freedom.

Presently Kennet put on his cap and leather jacket. Carefully, so that Grandfather would not notice, he got a loaf of bread from the cupboard box, a scrap of dried meat from the shelf. He opened the door then and slipped out.

On the porch's narrow step was Toby, the black hound. At sight of his master, the big fellow reared up on hind legs, barked joyously and began the comical dance which Kennet had taught him.

"No, Toby," Kennet said gravely. "This isn't the time for tricks."

Toby had the most beautiful eyes in the world and a wide mouth stretched in an incessant, amiable grin. He had intelligence, too, beneath that satiny black skull of his. At the boy's command he dropped down obediently on four feet again, wagging his tail.

The dog beside him, Kennet walked to the river and stood for a moment staring out over the ice-choked water. On the far shore, dim behind curtains of falling snow, were the rolling Pennsylvania hills. Nearer, on the Jersey side, were the piers and docks, deserted and idle.

Kennet turned his back on the town. He sought a path at the water's edge. For almost a mile he trudged, winding with the river through thickets of rustling, bare-branched trees and snow-shrouded bushes, reaching at last a clearing where nestled a sturdy wooden shed with peaked roof and little windows.

Over the door was a sign. Kennet read it sorrow-fully: "K. Strawn & Son, Carpenters." "K. Strawn?"— that was Grandfather, so ill and feeble. "Son"—that was Father, dear Father, far from home now, serving in the Continental Army. And there was no carpentry work done here these days.

Yet the shed did hold treasure even now, and Kennet must come occasionally like this to visit it. The shed housed his boat, the roomy, iron-keeled craft which

Grandfather and Father had built for him two years ago. *The Madcap*—that was her splendid name, lettered on her stern with yellow paint; and many a fine trip up and down the Delaware had Kennet taken in her. But that, of course, was before the war. Now *The Madcap* was propped, high and dry, on blocks within the shed walls. He didn't know when she would be sailed again.

He unlocked the door and swung it on its rusty hinges. The interior of the shed was gloomy with shadows, chill and bleak. He lighted a candle; his breath formed a little steamy cloud above the orange flame. He set the candle on a chest and bent over his boat. With a cloth he brushed dust from the seats and polished the metal strips on the rudder. But all this he did absently. Really, he was listening, waiting; and soon he heard what he listened for—a faint yet distinct scratching on the windowpane.

A signal.

Kennet strode to the door, pushed it cautiously ajar. A man entered. It was he, the ragged stranger, the wanderer Kennet had met yesterday in the woods, who was so hollow-eyed, starved and mysterious. In the circle of candlelight, the man and the boy faced each other. The man was first to speak.

"So, you came!" His voice was deep and musical. "I was afraid you'd forget."

"No, I couldn't forget my solemn promise."

"And did you bring me food?"

"A snack." Kennet drew the bread and meat from his pocket. "We had nothing else."

"Excellent, my boy!" The man's eyes gleamed. "A feast!" Throwing himself on a bench, he ate ravenously.

Watching, Kennet realized how hungry this stranger must be, and wondered how many hours had passed since his last meal. A great many, probably. The man glanced up and encountered the boy's steady, sober gaze. He smiled and wiped his mouth on the back of one red, frostbitten hand.

"As delicious a dinner as I ever had," he said, stooping to caress Toby, to stroke the long velvety ears. "I thank you for your kindness."

Kennet nodded courteously. "You are welcome."

"Sit down." As the boy took a place on the bench, the man said, "Why have you befriended me? You don't know me, never laid eyes on me until twenty-four hours ago."

"It's Christmas," Kennet answered simply.

"And you observe the day with charity?"

"Yes. I know you are deserving. You are not a tramp—even though your clothes are so torn and dirty."

"My clothes *are* shabby, aren't they?" He flipped the sleeve of his threadbare coat. "But they'll do. I don't go about much in society. You didn't mention to anyone that you saw me?" He paused anxiously.

"Not even to my grandfather."

"Good! It's absolutely necessary that I keep under cover. Much depends on it. You'd never have seen me yesterday, if I hadn't been near perishing for food. But there you were, on the river path—and there was I, peeping out. Remember? And in a moment we had spoken, were talking like comrades, well-met! And you were promising to feed me."

Kennet leaned forward. "I think," he said, "you are a soldier."

"A soldier?" The man flushed. "Now why should you think——"

"My father is a soldier, and if he is hungry today, I should like to believe that someone, somewhere, is feeding——"

But here Kennet paused, for the man was frowning, putting an admonishing finger to his lips. What was that noise at the door? Why did Toby bristle and growl?

The noise again. A stamping of feet, an angry shouting. "Open! Open, in the King's name!"

The King's name? An enemy, then? A Hessian? Kennet tiptoed to the window. Yes, outside in the snow bulked a stalwart figure, a Hessian, uniformed and armed.

"Open!" With his sword, the Hessian pounded the shed door.

Kennet's breath fluttered in his throat. "What shall we do?" he whispered.

"Open, and say you are alone." Swift as lightning, the ragged stranger leaped into *The Madcap,* flung himself down and crawled under a strip of canvas. He was hidden; he would not be seen.

Slowly Kennet went to the door, unlocked it; he was almost thrown over backward by the violence of the Hessian's rushing entrance. He braced himself before the rude intruder; he waited.

"What are you doing here? Who are you?"

"Kennet Strawn. I live in Trenton with my grandfather. This is his shop."

"Who is with you?" The words were curt, accusing.

"I am alone."

"Nonsense! The door was bolted. You were speaking to someone. You came here to meet someone. Where is he?"

"No, no——"

The Hessian grimaced. Scornfully, with the toe of his shiny boot, he indicated crumbs which had fallen to the floor. "Someone has dined here."

"I carried a bit of lunch in my pocket."

The Hessian lunged and grasped the boy by the shoulder, shook him fiercely. "You lie! You're sheltering a spy. You'll pay dear for this!"

At that very instant, Toby decided to have a part in the scene. Toby had been snarling, barking. Now, jaws wide, he dashed at the ruffian who threatened his beloved master. The dog's sharp teeth caught the man's leg above the heavy boot, sank in through cloth, found the flesh. With oaths and a howl of rage and pain, the Hessian released Kennet.

"You beast!" He kicked. He struck out with his fist. He whipped the sword from his belt. The terrible, glistening blade swept upward——

"Oh, please!" Kennet moaned. "Please don't kill Toby!"

The blade poised, descended in an arc—an arc that was abruptly halted. The sword was thrust aside, clat-

tered to the floor, as the Hessian swayed and struggled in a pair of steel-like arms.

It happened so quickly, the agile leap of the ragged stranger from his canvas cover, the Hessian's astonished outcry. And then they were lurching, tumbling, all over the room, in and out of shadow, the two big men, while Kennet gasped and Toby barked wildly.

The Hessian, after his first surprise, fought like a tiger. At last, he was subdued, he yielded.

"Quick!" the stranger muttered. "A rope. A rope."

Kennet fumbled in a chest, dragged forth a length of stout rope. They bound the Hessian with it; they rolled him into a corner.

"Now I must be off!" The stranger was mopping at his forehead, which was grimy and streaked with blood. "Not a minute to lose now!"

Kennet stepped back to view the limp figure of the enemy. "He isn't—isn't dead, is he?"

"No. He's not badly hurt. But he'll be quiet for a few hours. Then he'll rouse and spread the alarm. You must go home to your grandfather—and I must get away."

"Why did you jump up? He'd never have noticed you."

"Lie there like a stick of wood and let him mistreat you and kill your dog? Oh, no! No, my friend." He patted Toby's sleek head. "I must get away," he repeated and, his frown deepening, he pointed to *The Madcap*. "Whose boat is this?"

"Boat?" Kennet was startled at the change of subject. "Why—why, she's mine."

"Yours, eh? Want to sell her?" He laughed on a queer note. "I've got to have this boat. I can't explain, but—well, if you won't sell her, I'll steal her."

"Steal?" Kennet echoed, dismayed. "You'd steal my boat?"

"Yes. Oh, I'm an odd fellow, no doubt of it. Here!" He dug into his pocket, extracted a handful of coins. "Money."

Kennet's brain was reeling. The events of the past hour had marched so rapidly—and certainly there was no understanding them! He felt as if he were in the midst of a crazy sort of dream where nobody behaved naturally. But he was sure of one thing: he couldn't take money from this gallant, tattered wanderer who had risked detection, perhaps his life, for him and for Toby.

The Madcap; he loved her; he couldn't sell her. He thought very hard and arrived at a decision.

"Well?" The man was jangling the coins. "Well? Am I to be a purchaser or a thief?"

Kennet swallowed a huge lump in his throat. "Take the boat. I'll give her to you—for Christmas." Hadn't he been wishing all day for the opportunity to give a Christmas present?

The man bowed. "You'll never regret your generosity. You'll help me move her?"

They worked then like beavers, knocking the blocks from under *The Madcap,* straining every muscle to get her out of the shed, down the slope to the river. The snow aided them; though it made their footing insecure, it formed a smooth surface on which the iron keel glided like a sled on runners. Once Kennet, pausing, remarked breathily that the river was full of floating ice, it was scarcely navigable, escape would be easier by way of the woods. But the stranger only laughed; he said he needed a boat, *this* boat—and he didn't mind ice.

Dusk, finally, and *The Madcap* launched, and her new owner bidding farewell to the old!

"Good-by, my lad. God bless you."

"Good-by," Kennet quavered. He was tired, bewildered, the afternoon had been so crowded with excitement—and perhaps he hadn't acted wisely. "Can't —can't you tell me *anything* about yourself?"

The stranger was standing in the boat; he looked erect, soldierly. "I'll tell you this: you think you've given me a Christmas token—really, it's for someone else. For a great man, the greatest in the world today, a man who guides your fate, and mine, and all America's. This Christmas present will be delivered to him!" He smiled into the boy's puzzled face. "Hurry home. Be silent about our adventure—and don't be amazed at anything you hear!"

Early on the morning of December twenty-sixth, 1776, while the Hessian troops in Trenton dozed after their drinking and hilarious celebration of the night before, General George Washington and his men advanced upon the town. They entered by two roads, overwhelming and seizing the garrison. For hours the streets echoed with the roar of musket and cannon—and then the Hessians surrendered.

Grandfather, huddled close to the fire, was trying to piece together shreds of rumor and gossip into a logical story.

"They say he came across the Delaware, a few boats pushing through the ice. They say a spy has been here in the neighborhood for several days, obtaining boats by one means or another; and some of 'em splintered and crashed in midstream—and some crossed in safety."

Kennet was kneeling to mend the logs, shielding his face with his palm. *The Madcap,* had she made the crossing safely? Oh, he hoped so! And what if General Washington had been *The Madcap's* passenger—that great man, the greatest in the world, riding to victory in Kennet Strawn's bonny boat!

"The spy, Grandfather? Was he—taken?"

"They say not. They say he's one of the General's

trusted officers. A gentleman. A hero." Grandfather fondled Toby's velvet ears. "Now the tide has turned. God is with us and we will win. I may not last to see the end, myself, for I am so old. But freedom will come; it's on the way, in the air." He smiled happily. "Now I am content to die."

But Kennet did not want to die. No, no! This morning, as never before, he wanted to live—for his country.

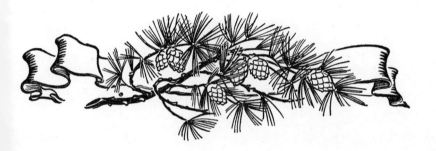

Sky-Fallen Peace

Christmas in the Northwest Territory

Josephine E. Phillips

"It won't be much like Christmas without Father," the boy complained. "I don't see why the garrison has to keep him hunting and trapping forever."

"Oh, yes, you do. It's because he's the best hunter in the whole Northwest Territory, and the soldiers have to have food." His mother tried to make her reply light and laughing, though she wasn't very happy herself. "If Christmas is hard for us, David, think how it must be for him, off in that little hut alone. If only you were a little older, I'd send you to him with a pumpkin pie——"

"Could I, Mother? Could I go? I'm old enough. A pumpkin pie! Oh, won't he be pleased?"

"But it's twenty miles, and if there should be snow——"

"But there won't be snow, Mother. Why, I—I'm sure there won't be snow. There was only a teeny bit all last winter. And twenty miles is nothing. A day's journey!"

"There might be an unfriendly Indian——"

"Pooh! You talk as though there hadn't been any peace treaty signed. As though Long Foot or Little Foot might pop out at me from behind a tree any minute. The rangers haven't seen their moccasin prints for months and months. His tribesmen say that Long Foot went on a journey to the Northland, and Little Foot disappeared soon after. But no one knows; they were so strange a pair, known only for their footprints, and their mischief. But I guess there isn't any Indian could catch me, anyhow. Who was it won four foot races on the last garrison holiday? Please, Mother, start baking that pumpkin pie!"

So it was that next morning before daybreak David set out to carry Christmas greeting to his hunter-father. Besides Mother's huge pumpkin pie, carefully covered and carried in a thin board box, there was a new soft deerskin cap, all warmly lined with bits of old wool, re-knitted by Hannah. And little Sally, not to be outdone by the generosity of the rest, insisted on tucking into the knapsack her choicest possession, a bead-and-shell belt which David had skillfully made for her the previous winter, a copy of the gay peace-treaty belt given to the garrison by the Delaware Indian chiefs.

The boy's own provisions were simple—frozen porridge to thaw out by a campfire, and dried venison to chew on. And his heart was even lighter than his knapsack! With Father happy in their remembrance of him, it would be Christmas after all.

A little like the New England Christmases, too, for in spite of his prophecy snow had begun falling steadily, drearily, some time in the night. Now it lay over the trail in a puffy blanket, two inches thick. David grinned to himself. No wonder the little gray squirrels had started south that fall, swimming the Ohio, hurrying to warmer regions; and no wonder the corn husks had been thick and tough, if they knew that this was the kind of a winter it was going to be!

He swung on and on, and was past the Forks where the main trail led off to the salt lick, before sunrise. Such a sunrise! The snow clouds seemed to drift away from the east just long enough to give him a peep at the glorious disk as it made every branch, every leafless vine, a thing of rosy beauty for a moment. Then the clouds swept back and all was still and gray once more.

The trail grew fainter as snow covered the path. Here and there David was misled to right or left and had to retrace his steps. He only laughed aloud, for love of the adventure. On and on. It was Christmas Eve and before many hours he would be warming his toes by his father's campfire, telling him all the news of the garrison, all the gossip of the river-boats. He would feel very grown up sitting by that campfire, with maybe a bowl of fresh bear's-oil——

That made him hungry. He chose a spot protected from the wind, gathered dead branches and brushed the snow from them. Then, by means of a flint and a cherished bit of tow-string, he kindled a fire and thawed out his porridge. My, but it tasted good! It made him realize how cold and hungry he had been. But he did not loiter. As soon as he had eaten, he warmed two little flat stones, one for each pocket, to keep his hands from getting numb. Then he stamped out the fire and started off again.

The dim trail soon left the river bottoms and led through denser forests onto a ridge. Twelve miles of his journey was done, but it was mid-afternoon. And twilight came early. David did not relish the idea of spending the night out, this near to his goal without reaching it.

He started down the ridge at an easy dogtrot, risking the possibility of losing his way. Just as he reached the shelter of a little hollow, a low wail came to his ears. He stopped short.

What could it be? Not a baby, off in this wilderness. Yet it sounded for all the world like Sally, when she was younger and had bumped her nose on a rough log. A captive, perhaps? But the Indians had promised to take no more captives.

Before he could decide whether he ought to investigate the sound he fairly stumbled upon the source of it. He found the two bright black eyes of a little red-and-brown papoose looking at him from the depths of a bear-skin hood.

David saw in a moment what had happened. The baby, strapped in its carrier, had been left by its mother on the branch of a tree. The wind must have blown the strange cradle into the snow, or perhaps the papoose had been too lively, and had kicked himself down. Anyhow, there he was, out of the carrier, and nearly out of his deerskin blanket. His legs were still tangled in his trappings, bare and purple-cold from the snow.

David's first thought was to leave him squalling there. Time on the trail was precious, every minute of it. Yet there was no telling when the Indian mother would return. If it were little Sally lost out here in the snow——

With a heavy sigh the boy set down his knapsack and went to work to make the baby more comfortable. It wasn't an easy job. The straps of the carrier proved too complicated for him to unpuzzle, and it was some time before he could get him to sit still in his little blanket. At last, to amuse him while he was gathering brush for a fire, David reached into his knapsack and brought out the bead treaty-belt.

The papoose was delighted with it for a few minutes, then he began biting it so hungrily that David began to worry lest he swallow the beads.

"And goodness knows, if I've got to stay here all night being nurse girl I don't want you yelling with a stomach-ache because of them!" David explained. "If you're hungry——"

He broke off the remnants of his own porridge,

warmed them on a stick, and fed them one by one to the starving, greedy babe. Soon he became alarmed at the child's evident capacity.

"See here, you little rascal! You must be looking for that pumpkin pie. But you shan't get it, today, not if I can help myself. Say, I've a mind to pack you up and take you along with me. If your shiftless squaw-mother doesn't care any more about you than——"

The boy's speech, delivered in a sing-song tone intended to act somewhat as a soothing lullaby, was interrupted by a series of short expressive grunts.

Surprise, displeasure, then relief and satisfaction, were in the little squaw's voice as she laid down her heavy burden of deer carcass and snatched up her papoose. She examined him swiftly for signs of ill-treatment, then hustled him into his carrier and strapped him to the safety of her back, while the papoose himself yelled lustily all the time and brandished the treaty-belt about her head to show his disapproval of thus losing his freedom unexpectedly.

As soon as she could listen, David explained in simple words and signs his finding of the baby in the snow, and warming and feeding it. The mother was very attentive and then to his great surprise began questioning him, in fairly good English.

"Where white boy going?"

"To his father, a great hunter in the Black Forest, with gifts."

She puzzled over that. "Gifts! To his father? Why?"

"Because it is Christmas tomorrow."

"Christmas!" He thought she was excited over pronouncing the strange hissing syllables.

"Because of a little Baby's birthday," he explained slowly. "A little Baby, Jesus."

He looked about him at the swift-gathering darkness, and a wave of homesickness, loneliness, swept over him. If it hadn't been for this interruption he might even now be at his father's campfire. Perhaps, if he hurried——

He began picking up his things and did not notice the strange gleam in the little squaw's eyes as he spoke the words, "Baby Jesus." He did not notice, either, the tall gaunt, brown figure that emerged from the forest gloom and stood by him in the circle of firelight, glowering.

"Ugh!" came a menacing grunt. David turned in alarm, but already the squaw had stepped between the two.

She spoke to the man in short sentences. She had to hold her head way back in order to look up into his face. David's glance shifted down to the moccasined feet of the pair. His so long, hers so tiny, hardly seven inches long! Just like——

Terror seized the boy. Just like the mysterious Long Foot and his friend Little Foot, the pair who had wrought mischief time and again in the settlements down-river. It must be they, and Little Foot, the inseparable friend, was really Long Foot's squaw. A brave, fearless, loyal squaw she must be, too, for an Indian like Long Foot to let her remain with him on the hunt, or on the warpath. Oh, he would have much to tell the garrison when he got home! But how should he get home?

Fleet-footed though he was, escape was out of the question with night falling. No. He had done their papoose no harm. Surely they would not mistreat him unless he showed a faint heart.

The consultation with Little Foot over, the Indian advanced, extending his hand in friendly fashion.

"White boy help papoose. Long Foot white boy's friend. Be white boy's father."

"Oh, but I want to see my own father!" the white boy cried.

The Indian frowned and shook his head.

"Where? Who?"

"In the forest, two-three-hour's walk," David answered. "White boy's father great hunter, Andrew Kerr. Sure Great Warrior Long Foot knows Hunter Kerr."

The man's frown deepened. "White hunters kill red brothers' game, take red brothers' forest, hunting grounds, while Long Foot away in Northland. Long Foot punish. Long Foot take Hunter Kerr captive, one-two days ago——"

Suddenly he stopped speaking. A dangling object had fallen at his feet. He stooped and picked it up, spread it flat with fingers that trembled, turned it over and over.

His eyes grew round with awe, half fear.

"See! The peace belt of my fathers! Sky-fallen. A sign from the Great Spirit." He held up the miniature belt for his squaw to behold. "Long Foot had forgotten the peace of his fathers."

When they saw how reverently he viewed the trifle, Little Foot tried to explain that the papoose had dropped it, and David tried to explain that he had given it to him for a plaything. But Long Foot would not listen.

He was confident that he had received a sign from the Great Spirit, a sign he must obey. He would go and release his captive. He would remember the treaty of his fathers with their brothers the white men. In a moment he was gone, noiselessly, into the forest.

Eagerly David waited. Could it be that Sally's gift had saved his father and himself from captivity? Would Long Foot return?

Little Foot seated herself by the campfire, across from him.

"This Baby Jesus, tell me the Baby Jesus story. My mother, father, they were Christians. My village, all Christian. Our teacher white missionary from over the Great Water, beyond the rising sun. Some day Long Foot will be Christian. Tell me Jesus story."

So while the little papoose slept, and the only sound of the forest was the sputtering of snowflakes as they slipped into the fire, David told the old, old Christmas story to his new friend. Never had it seemed so beautiful or meant so much, that message of "Peace on Earth, Good will toward Men."

He was hardly done when he found himself caught up, knapsack and all, in the close embrace of his father, while Long Foot and Little Foot stood by, approving.

The boy wriggled himself free.

"You've squished it, Father. I don't really mind, but you must have squished it."

"Squished what?"

"The huge pumpkin pie I was bringing you for Christmas. See!"

In a twinkling they had the pastry out. It was frozen so hard that it wasn't hurt.

Around the campfire they shared it, with true good will, Long Foot and Little Foot, Hunter Kerr and his son.

A Trade=About Christmas

A Story of 1862

Frances Cavanah

Mrs. Sterling was warming herself before the fireplace after a long drive from Frederick where she had gone to take a basket of delicacies to the soldiers in the hospital. She was very tired, but when Sarah rushed into the parlor, her cheeks pale and streaked with tears, she drew the child down beside her on the sofa and heard her story.

"Oh, Mother! I added a postscript to my last letter to Father, and told him he'd better come home for Christmas or I wouldn't love him any more. And now he's on the march and maybe I'll never see him again and——"

Mrs. Sterling shook her head sadly, for she had not known before of the impetuous postscript. Sarah, choked by sobs, handed her the letter she had just received from her father, Captain Sterling, a Union officer during the trying days of the War between the States.

"My dear little girl," Mrs. Sterling read. "I know you will be brave, when I tell you that I cannot be with you for the holidays. Remember, our disappointment is as nothing, compared to the disappointment of an army that must spend Christmas away from their own firesides. Try to think of that, Sarah, and make a happy Christmas for some soldier besides your father. I shall be on the march for several weeks with no definite address, and cannot receive a box from you. But some other soldier can.

"With love to my little girl, who, I know, loves me as much as she ever did, Father."

"Why not do as Father suggests?" said Mrs. Sterling. "If we send a box to the Sanitary Commission, they'll see that some soldier gets it."

"I'd like to pack a box," Sarah answered, growing quieter in the circle of her mother's arm, "but I'd like it even better if we could see a soldier enjoy his Christmas face to face."

"I wish we could have a few guests for Christmas, but right now there aren't any soldiers near enough to come. Still—" Mrs. Sterling smiled. "I think I'll have to have a talk with Miss Jenny."

Miss Jenny was the girls' beloved young teacher, and it was she who had organized the Children's Aid Society among them, to knit and work for the soldiers. When they met the following Saturday afternoon, she had an announcement.

"I'm afraid the soldiers over in Frederick Hospital are going to have a dreary time this Christmas, unless the people of Frederick County come to the rescue. They're feeling very discouraged, for though most of them are better they're not able to go home or to rejoin their regiments."

"We girls are part of the people of Frederick County," said Sarah. "Can't we do something?"

"That's exactly what your mother thought. The ladies of the town are serving the men a Christmas dinner, but they'd appreciate some homemade cookies, especially if you girls delivered them yourselves on Christmas afternoon. Then they're sadly in need of reading matter, and I know many of our neighbors have magazines and books they'll gladly give, if we will just collect them."

The girls could keep silent no longer. Ellen thought the soldiers would enjoy a Christmas tree, and Sarah suggested they would prefer gingerbread men to cookies. It was Amanda's idea that the girls should dress in red, white and blue to make things seem patriotic.

"Let's give an entertainment for the soldiers," said Sarah.

"We can speak pieces and sing carols and—why, we could give a tableau, too."

The days that followed were days of flurrying

snows and ice-encrusted roads. Frost changed the farms into havens of white beauty; and in the midst of war Sarah felt a strange new sense of peace.

She hitched old Robin to the sleigh to canvass her neighbors and brought back home a goodly supply of magazines and books. She practiced Christmas carols as she knitted and rehearsed the piece she would speak at the entertainment.

"Why can't we have a moving tableau?" asked Sarah at their last meeting before Christmas.

"Silly," said Amanda, "it wouldn't be a tableau if you moved."

"Well, then, a moving *picture*."

"Humph! Who ever heard of a moving picture?"

Sarah grew very red trying to explain. "What I mean is this. When I recite 'Lady Clare,' why couldn't the rest of you dress up like Lady Clare, Lord Ronald, and old Alice the nurse, and act it out? Only, of course, you wouldn't say anything—I'd do all the talking."

[133]

"That's called a pantomime," said Miss Jenny kindly. "It would make a nice feature for our exercises the last day of school, but we haven't time to make any special costumes now."

Sarah swallowed her disappointment bravely. She could just see Ellen, with her fair hair falling over her shoulders, playing the part of Lady Clare. She would wear a long white trailing robe and afterwards throw a cape over it for a russet gown. Amanda's costume as Lord Ronald might be more difficult, but Harriet would make a lovable old nurse with very little fixing. So enthusiastic did she become over her plans for the last day of school that she almost forgot the program they were to give in a few days. Conundrum, one of the small darkies on the farm, drove over after her in the carriage, and in him she found a willing audience.

"Don't you see how it would be, Conundrum? When I say,

> 'I trow they did not part in scorn,
> Lovers long betrothed were they,'

Ellen will look up at Amanda so trustingly, and she'll be a little wistful, too, because she can hardly wait for the morrow to come."

"Lak dis?" said Conundrum, making a pillow for his black little cheek on his very black little hands.

"Well, something like that," Sarah admitted, trying not to laugh. "Then when Alice the nurse tells Lady Clare that she is not really the Earl's daughter but her own child, Ellen will stand up very straight and act dramatic when I say, 'Falsely, falsely, have ye done.' The nurse will cry then, and Lady Clare will repent and kiss her, because the nurse is really her mother, and Alice will lay her hand upon her head and bless her ere she goes. Then when Lady Clare meets Lord Ronald——"

The narrative continued, Sarah, in spite of an abundance of wraps, giving an animated impersonation of the three characters. Conundrum imitated every move she made. "Laws-a-mighty, Miss Sarah, yo' sho am sma't."

Sarah found his praise gratifying. "Well, at least, I'm going to speak a piece for the soldiers, and then maybe the last day of school I can say it again and the girls can act it out."

"Ah wish *Ah* could see the sojers," said Conundrum wistfully.

Christmas Eve was a busy day for Miss Jenny and her pupils. Each worked in her own home and Sarah had a whole regiment of gingerbread men before she finished her share of the baking. She was still lingering over their early Christmas dinner the next day, when the sound of sleigh bells rang clearly through the frosty air.

"Oh, I didn't expect them to come so soon," she cried, hurrying into her wraps. Then she picked up the basket, in which she had packed a quantity of magazines and books, and, staggering under their weight, sped down the front walk to the bobsled where Miss Jenny and her pupils waited. Not until she was a good ten miles away did she realize that she had left her gingerbread men behind.

"We can't possibly turn back," said Miss Jenny. "But never mind, dear. The other girls have brought cookies, and there will be enough to go around."

But Sarah was not so easily consoled, thinking of how jolly the gingerbread men would have looked hanging on the Christmas tree. She was almost sure she had packed them on top of the magazines and books.

The sleigh drew up before two large stone buildings, that had been erected back in the time of George Washington. Long wooden barracks had been added, as the number of patients increased, and in one of these, the girls found a goodly number of men assembled to hear their entertainment. They cheered lustily when the girls opened their program with "The Star Spangled Banner," and followed this with several popular songs.

The tableaux did not meet with such a gratifying response. Ellen, holding the American flag, looked very lovely as Miss Columbia, and Harriet, busy with her knitting, was "The Girl I Left Behind Me." There was only a sputter of polite applause, and Sarah thought a little uneasily of the piece she was to speak.

Amanda, conscious of the lagging interest, put all the eloquence at her command into "The Boy Stood on the Burning Deck." For all her effort, though, it was a failure, and though the men tried to look interested, they only succeeded in looking bored. Sarah was glad that "Lady Clare" at least had a happy ending.

Still, it was not an easy experience, when it came her turn to stand up before them and read in their faces

the look which so plainly said, "Mehercule! Must we go
through another one?"

Bravely she began:

"It was the time when lilies blow,
And clouds are highest up in air,
Lord Ronald brought a lily white doe
To give his cousin, Lady Clare."

The men sat up eagerly. They leaned forward, and
interest was written on their faces. More confidently,
Sarah began the second stanza:

"I trow they did not part in scorn;
Lovers long betrothed were they;
They two will wed the morrow morn;
God's blessing on the day.
" 'He does not love me for my birth,
Nor for my lands so broad and fair;
He loves me for my own true worth,
And that is well,' said Lady Clare."

The soldiers' eyes gleamed with something more
than interest now. There was a chuckle in the back of
the room, and two or three of the men were openly grin-
ning. Sarah grew very red, paused a moment, then
struggled on.

"In there came old Alice the nurse,
Said, 'Who was this that went from thee?'
'It was my cousin,' said Lady Clare,
'Tomorrow he weds with me.'

" 'O God be thanked!' said Alice the nurse,
   'That all comes round so just and fair.
Lord Ronald is heir of all your lands,
   And you are not the Lady Clare.' "

Sarah had hoped that her audience would be impressed by this important statement; but she had not expected it to shout with mirth. She looked at her schoolmates and saw that they were laughing, too. Even Miss Jenny found it hard to keep a straight face. She smiled at Sarah encouragingly and motioned for her to go on. It was one of the hardest things that Sarah ever did, but she obeyed.

What had happened was that Conundrum had opened the door behind her and had entered, carrying the forgotten package. He was wrapped in his mammy's huge plaid shawl, and only his thin little black face protruded from the folds. He was pinched with cold, but his wish to see the soldiers was gratified after a long drive along the icy roads with only Teaser, the dog, for company. The grateful little darky grinned his own peculiar grin that belonged to Conundrum and to no one else, and it was this that had caused the first quickening of interest on the part of the audience.

Conundrum set down his basket and blew upon his hands. Then began the slow process of unwinding the voluminous shawl, and he emerged just about the time that Sarah reached her third stanza. Suddenly he became aware that it was his own beloved little mistress who

was reciting and that she was saying "Lady Clare." He knew all the gestures—Miss Sarah had shown him and, moreover, she had been wishing for someone to act it out. She had reached the line, "He loves me for my own true worth," when, almost unconscious of what he was doing, Conundrum laid his hand over his heart just as Sarah had done. In his attempt to look as soulful as she had, he rolled his eyes to heaven.

There was a muffled chuckle in the back of the room, but it was all the encouragement that Conundrum needed. He was quick to sense the appreciation of his audience, and as Sarah recited he acted the part of each character in turn.

Sarah was growing more and more bewildered by

the slowly mounting laughter, but again Miss Jenny nodded for her to go on. Bravely she began:

> " 'If I'm a beggar born,' she said,
>   'I will speak out, for I dare not lie.
> Pull off, pull off the brooch of gold,
>   And fling the diamond necklace by.' "

Conundrum rubbed his woolly pate in perplexity, but only for a moment. He ripped off one of his few remaining shirt buttons and flung it away with a disdainful gesture.

"She clad herself in a russet gown," said Sarah, and Conundrum, wrapping the plaid shawl around him, tripped across the floor as he thought a high-born lady would. The next stanza taxed his ingenuity still further, but the virus of success had crept into his blood. Like many another actor, he was determined not to disappoint his audience. He remembered Teaser contentedly gnawing a bone just inside the main entrance to the hospital.

The mist in Sarah's eyes blotted out the sight of her hilarious audience, but her voice was still firm.

> "The lily-white doe Lord Ronald had brought
>   Leapt up from where she lay,
> Dropt her head in the maiden's hand,
>   And followed her all the way."

Conundrum puckered his lips and whistled. In bounded Teaser, his plumy tail sticking straight up into the air. But he did not drop his head into Conundrum's palm—he made a dash for Sarah.

"Go on and finish," said Miss Jenny under cover of the laughter. "It's the hit of the day."

Sarah was quick to see the joke and to the accompaniment of Conundrum's animated pantomime, the audience learned that the love of Lord Ronald and Lady Clare came to a happy ending.

"Well, little lady," said one bronzed soldier, as she stopped by his chair a few minutes later with her basket. "I have a little gal about your age."

"I reckon she's missing you just about as much as I'm missing my father this Christmas," said Sarah.

"I reckon so, but she'll be glad to know that a little gal like you has brightened up the day for me."

This remark was repeated to Sarah several times as she went up and down the room, and she felt indeed as though she were seeing the soldiers enjoy their Christmas face to face. It had turned out to be a most satisfactory afternoon, but this did not prevent her taking one small offender to task.

"Ah ain't done nuffin wrong, Miss Sarah. Yo' mammy foun' yo' cookies on de kitchen table and done tol' me to bring em to yo'—dat's all."

"But, Conundrum, I just know I put that package of gingerbread men on top the books."

Conundrum puckered his lips in a whistle.

"Listen here, Conundrum. Did you move them?"

The whistling grew louder.

"You must answer me. I won't tell your mammy."

"Ah 'spects Ah did," said Conundrum.

Sarah understood it all now. He had wished to see

the soldiers and he knew if Sarah left her gingerbread men behind, he would in all probability be sent after her to deliver them. And by so doing he had turned the program into a huge success.

"It's all right this time, Conundrum, but don't you ever dare do a thing like that again."

Conundrum grinned. This was the way Miss Sarah's scoldings usually ended.

Before they left the girls sang again for the soldiers. Deep male voices joined with theirs in "Holy Night," and "Hark, the Herald Angels Sing," and when twilight crept softly in the windows it found a group of quiet men, more contented than they had been for weeks.

Mrs. Sterling gave her consent for Sarah to sit up and watch the Old Year die. Slavery was dying with it, for on the morrow—January first, 1863—Abraham Lincoln's Emancipation Proclamation was to go into effect. She felt very solemn, sitting by the fire through the long evening hours.

Just before midnight Jake drove Mother home from town where she had been attending a meeting at the church. She held out a letter from Father. Sarah laughed happily as she opened it.

"My dear little girl: I hope that you and Mother spent as happy a Christmas as I did. At first, it seemed very dreary, when I thought of Sarah so faraway. My men were feeling just as blue as I was, when an agent of the Sanitary Commission drove up with a wagon filled with Christmas boxes. There was one for me, and when

I opened it, not only did I find a roast turkey, a knitted scarf and all the goodies that go with Christmas, but I found this note which I am enclosing. A little girl your age had packed the box."

Sarah dropped her father's letter and picked up the note he had enclosed. It came from Philadelphia.

"Dear Unknown Soldier," she read. "I hope you like this box I've packed for you. My father is a soldier, too, but he's in the hospital at Frederick, Maryland——."

"Mother!" Sarah looked up, her eyes shining. "She must be the daughter of one of those men who told me he had a little girl my age. She made the day happy for my father and I made it happy for hers. Why, it was a regular trade-about Christmas."

Mother smiled gently and held up a warning finger. "Hark!" she said.

The church bells in the town were ringing and the music came to them, soft, and clear, across the frozen fields. The year, 1863, had come.

A Miserable, Merry Christmas

A Real Adventure in California in the Seventies

Lincoln Steffens

What interested me in our new neighborhood was not the school, nor the room I was to have in the house all to myself, but the stable which was built back of the house. My father let me direct the making of a stall, a little smaller than the other stalls, for my pony, and I prayed and hoped and my sister Lou believed that that meant that I would get the pony, perhaps for Christmas. I pointed out to her that there were three other stalls and no horses at all. This I said in order that she should answer it. She could not. My father, sounded, said that some day we might have horses and a cow; meanwhile the stable added to the value of a house. "Some day" is a pain to a boy who lives in and knows only "now." My good little sisters, to comfort me, remarked that Christmas was coming, but Christmas was always coming and grownups were always talking about it, asking you what you wanted and then giving you what they wanted you to have. Though everybody knew what I wanted, I told them all again. My mother knew that I told God, too, every night. I wanted a pony, and to make sure that they understood, I declared that I wanted nothing else.

"Nothing but a pony?" my father asked.

"Nothing," I said.

"Not even a pair of high boots?"

That was hard. I did want boots, but I stuck to the pony. "No, not even boots."

"Nor candy? There ought to be something to fill your stocking with, and Santa Claus can't put a pony into a stocking."

That was true, and he couldn't lead a pony down the chimney either. But no. "All I want is a pony," I said. "If I can't have a pony, give me nothing, nothing."

Now I had been looking myself for the pony I wanted, going to sales stables, inquiring of horsemen, and I had seen several that would do. My father let me "try" them. I tried so many ponies that I was learning fast to sit a horse. I chose several, but my father always found some fault with them. I was in despair. When Christmas was at hand I had given up all hope of a pony, and on Christmas Eve I hung up my stocking along with my sisters', of whom, by the way, I now had three. I haven't mentioned them or their coming because, you understand, they were girls, and girls, young girls, counted for nothing in my manly life. They did not mind me either; they were so happy that Christmas Eve that I caught some of their merriment. I speculated on what I'd get; I hung up the biggest stocking I had, and we all went reluctantly to bed to wait till morning. Not to sleep; not right away. We were told that we must not only sleep promptly, we must not wake up till seven-thirty the next morning—or if we did, we must not go to the fireplace for our Christmas. Impossible.

We did sleep that night, but we woke up at six A.M. We lay in our beds and debated through the open doors whether to obey till, say, half past six. Then we bolted. I don't know who started it, but there was a rush. We all disobeyed; we raced to disobey and get first to the fireplace in the front room downstairs. And there they were, the gifts, all sorts of wonderful things, mixed-up piles of presents; only, as I disentangled the mess, I saw that my stocking was empty; it hung limp; not a thing in it; and under and around it—nothing. My sisters had knelt down each by her pile of gifts; they were squealing with delight, till they looked up and saw me standing there in my nightgown with nothing. They left their piles to come to me and look with me at my empty place. Nothing. They felt my stocking: nothing.

I don't remember whether I cried at that moment, but my sisters did. They ran with me back to my bed,

and there we all cried till I became indignant. That
helped some. I got up, dressed, and driving my sisters
away, I went alone out into the yard, down to the stable,
and there, all by myself, I wept. My mother came out
to me by and by; she found me in my pony stall, sobbing
on the floor, and she tried to comfort me. But I heard
my father outside; he had come part way with her, and
she was having some sort of angry quarrel with him. She
tried to comfort me; besought me to come to breakfast.
I could not; I wanted no comfort and no breakfast. She
left me and went on into the house with sharp words
for my father.

I don't know what kind of breakfast the family had. My sisters said it was "awful." They were ashamed to enjoy their own toys. They came to me, and I was rude. I ran away from them. I went around to the front of the house, sat down on the steps, and, the crying over, I ached. I was wronged, I was hurt—I can feel now what I felt then, and I am sure that if one could see the wounds upon our hearts, there would be found still upon mine a scar from that terrible Christmas morning. And my father, the practical joker, he must have been hurt, too, a little. I saw him looking out of the window. He was watching me or something for an hour or two, drawing back the curtain ever so little lest I catch him, but I saw his face, and I think I can see now the anxiety upon it, the worried impatience.

After—I don't know how long—surely an hour or two—I was brought to the climax of my agony by the sight of a man riding a pony down the street, a pony and a brand-new saddle; the most beautiful saddle I ever saw, and it was a boy's saddle; the man's feet were not in the stirrups; his legs were too long. The outfit was perfect; it was the realization of all my dreams, the answer to all my prayers. A fine new bridle, with a light curb bit. And the pony! As he drew near, I saw that the pony was really a small horse, what we called an Indian pony, a bay, with black mane and tail, and one white foot and a white star on his forehead. For such a horse as that I would have given, I could have forgiven, anything.

But the man, a disheveled fellow with a blackened

eye and a fresh-cut face, came along, reading the numbers on the houses, and, as my hopes—my impossible hopes—rose, he looked at our door and passed by, he and the pony, and the saddle and the bridle. Too much. I fell upon the steps, and having wept before, I broke now into such a flood of tears that I was a floating wreck when I heard a voice.

"Say, kid," it said, "do you know a boy named Lennie Steffens?"

I looked up. It was the man on the pony, back again, at our horse block.

"Yes," I spluttered through my tears. "That's me."

"Well," he said, "then this is your horse. I've been looking all over for you and your house. Why don't you put your number where it can be seen?"

"Get down," I said, running out to him.

He went on saying something about "ought to have got here at seven o'clock; he told me to bring the nag here and tie him to your post and leave him for you . . ."

"Get down," I said.

He got down, and he boosted me up to the saddle. He offered to fit the stirrups to me, but I didn't want him to. I wanted to ride.

"What's the matter with you?" he said, angrily. "What you crying for? Don't you like the horse? He's a dandy, this horse. I know him of old. He's fine at cattle; he'll drive 'em alone."

I hardly heard, I could scarcely wait, but he persisted. He adjusted the stirrups, and then, finally, off I rode, slowly, at a walk, so happy, so thrilled, that I did not know what I was doing. I did not look back at the house or the man, I rode off up the street, taking note of everything—of the reins, of the pony's long mane, of the carved leather saddle. I had never seen anything so beautiful. And mine! I was going to ride up past Miss Kay's house. But I noticed on the horn of the saddle some stains like raindrops, so I turned and trotted home, not to the house but to the stable. There was the family, father, mother, sisters, all working for me, all happy. They had been putting in place the tools of my new business: blankets, currycomb, brush, pitchfork—everything, and there was hay in the loft.

"What did you come back so soon for?" somebody asked. "Why didn't you go on riding?"

I pointed to the stains. "I wasn't going to get my new saddle rained on," I said. And my father laughed. "It isn't raining," he said. "Those are not raindrops."

"They are tears," my mother gasped, and she gave my father a look which sent him off to the house. Worse still, my mother offered to wipe away the tears still running out of my eyes. I gave her such a look as she had given him, and she went off after my father, drying her own tears.

My sisters remained and we all unsaddled the pony, put on his halter, led him to his stall, tied and fed him. It began really to rain; so all the rest of that memorable day we curried and combed that pony. The girls plaited his mane, forelock, and tail, while I pitchforked hay to him and curried and brushed, curried and brushed. For a change we brought him out to drink; we led him up and down, blanketed like a race horse; we took turns at that. But the best, the most inexhaustible fun, was to clean him.

When we went reluctantly to our midday Christmas dinner, we smelt of horse, and my sisters had to wash their faces and hands. I was asked to, but I wouldn't, till my mother bade me look in the mirror. Then I washed up—quick. My face was caked with muddy lines of tears that had coursed over my cheeks to my mouth. Having washed away that shame, I ate my dinner, and as I ate I grew hungrier and hungrier. It was my first meal that day, and as I filled up on the turkey and the stuffing, the cranberries and the pies, the fruit and the nuts—as I swelled, I could laugh. My mother said I still choked and sobbed now and then, but I laughed, too; I saw and enjoyed my sisters' presents till—I had to go out and attend to my pony, who was there, really and truly there, the promise, the beginning, of a happy double life. And—I went and looked to make sure—there was the saddle, too, and the bridle.

But that Christmas, which my father had planned so carefully, was it the best or the worst I ever knew? He often asked me that; I never could answer as a boy. I think now that it was both. It covered the whole distance from broken-hearted misery to bursting happiness —too fast. A grownup could hardly have stood it.

Born is the King of Israel

An Old-Fashioned Christmas in New York

Ruth Sawyer

[Back in New York in the eighteen-nineties, while her parents were abroad, ten-year-old Lucinda Wyman spent a delightful year under the care of Miss Peters, one of her teachers. Roller skating up and down the streets, she made many friends, among them Tony, whose father owned a fruit stand; Patrolman M'Gonegal and Jerry Hanlon, also on the police force; Mr. Gilligan who drove a hansom cab; and a beautiful lady from Asia whom Lucinda called the Princess Zayda. There were other friends, too—Miss Nettie, sister of Miss

Peters; fat little Mrs. Caldwell and her dog Pyg-
malion; Miss Lucy, honey, as everyone called the
owner of the rooming house where Lucinda was
staying; and Mr. Night Owl, the newspaper re-
porter who slept by day and worked by night. Best
of all, there was Trinket, the tiny golden-haired
girl who lived on the floor above. Though her
father, Serge Browdowski, was a wonderful violin-
ist, Lucinda knew they were very poor and she
wanted to give Trinket a real Christmas.]—Editor's
note.

Snow came; first in flurries that melted away by
midday; then in a heavy, lazy falling of flakes that
covered window sills, pavements and street. The roller
skates were put away reluctantly in Lucinda's wardrobe;
leggings and overshoes came out of their wrappings, and
Lucinda looked with longing at a bright red sled in the
window of the little toy-stationery-and-tobacco shop on
Eighth Avenue. She wished she had it to take Trinket
riding in the snow. She thought about it and thought
about it and dreamed about it at night in the folding bed.

It cost a good deal of money, that sled. She couldn't
buy it, but she could do something else for Trinket. She
could have a tree for her. She talked it over first with
Miss Peters and Miss Nettie. "I'll have to go to Aunt
Emily's for Christmas Eve—same as usual. I guess I'll
have to keep on going there as long as I live—ninety
years, perhaps. The Waters girls, and the Brown girls
and the gazelles and I will be white tarlatan angels, just

as we've been since we could walk. And we'll sing carols and wave our star-wands and Aunt Emily will say, same as usual, 'When are you going to learn to be graceful, Lucinda?'" Lucinda ended with a giggle. "But on Christmas morning can't we have a special Christmas tree for Trinket—a little tree and make all the things for it, and have it a big surprise?"

She talked it over with Mrs. Browdowski one day when Trinket was out with her father; and discovered that Trinket had never had a tree in all the four years of her tiny life. So that made it more exciting than ever —to have for Trinket her very first tree! The more she thought about it the more positive she was that they couldn't keep all the fun of it to themselves—just she and Miss Peters and Miss Nettie. Miss Lucy, honey, must come, Mr. Night Owl, Lady Ross. And of course the Gilligans and Uncle Earle; and Aleda, down from the Gedney House; Tony, and perhaps he might bring the bambino. There was no end to the people she would like to invite.

She couldn't invite people to a Christmas tree and not have a present for everybody. She had spent all her allowance up to Saint Nicholas Day on THE TEMPEST. Where could she get money for presents? How —where—how—where? The silly old question ran around in her head like a kitten after a spool. If she could earn some money now!

She dropped in one afternoon to see Mrs. Caldwell and that charming old lady gave her her first idea. The snow was bad; the pavements slippery; she was afraid

of falling; Pygmalion was not getting out for his walk. "If you would come every day, my dear, then I wouldn't worry. He loves to go with you better than anyone else; and that would help toward your Christmas fund. You would be earning it."

"How perfectly glorious! It doesn't seem right to earn money so pleasantly. Mama never paid me to do anything except what I positively hated to do."

"That's too bad. I think money ought to be always earned pleasantly. Think of how much gayer the world would be if everybody went to work in the morning knowing he was going to do something he enjoyed doing all day!" As Mrs. Caldwell said it Lucinda thought she looked more than ever like the pictures of Queen Victoria, with her lace cap and her chunky chin and her sleepy, kind old eyes.

Afterwards she stopped at suite 207 and found her Princess Zayda very sad; and then all of a sudden very glad when she found who had come knocking at her door. "I have fresh Turkish candy for you and a bowl of litchi nuts. You will like, yes?"

So full was Lucinda with her news of earning money for Christmas that she could talk of nothing else. Twice, three times, the princess tried to put in a word and failed utterly. Not until Lucinda had run down like a clock did she discover that an idea like Mrs. Caldwell's could be carried like scarlet fever; only with pleasanter results. "Keep without moving, little Lucinda, and I speak. My 'usband say I talk the English very bad. Every day after you take the little dog for promenade, you shall come here and teach me the English. So—you like earn more money?"

After that, every day until Christmas, Lucinda was as busy as Mr. Gilligan with his hansom cab. At three she took Pygmalion out, putting on his blanket, sometimes his overshoes. For an hour she visited with her friends up and down Broadway; sometimes Aleda came with her and they talked of plays. Aleda knew hundreds of plays, it seemed, and she would tell the stories of them. Sometimes Lucinda went on Eighth Avenue, to renew acquaintance with Jerry Hanlon and see if Tony was minding the stand. She would go into the toy-stationery-and-tobacco shop and warm her feet and Pygmalion's toes beside the stove. It was very warm and comfortable inside. Mr. and Mrs. Schultz who kept the shop always made them welcome, and Lucinda usually bought a pennyworth of coltsfoot or licorice stick so as not to wear that welcome out. Another thing she always did; it made the Schultzes laugh and gave her a great deal of satisfaction. She went around the shop and undid all the fastenings on the jack-in-the-boxes. Out they would pop with a squeak, flap their silly hands, and grin at Lucinda. Lucinda would always grin back and say the same thing to each: "There, I bet you that feels good!"

Once Mrs. Schultz asked her: "Kindlein, why you the boxes open like so—always?" And Lucinda answered: "Oh, I don't know. I guess I like the squeak."

At four o'clock she was unblanketing Pygmalion in Mrs. Caldwell's room and telling everything that had happened. To the old lady's keen delight she made up and repeated as actual such conversations as she and Pygmalion had had together. One day it ran this wise, and in her own heart Lucinda had not meant it to sound more than nonsense:

"Pygmalion said, 'Lucinda, let's go round on Eighth Avenue and see that elegant red sled again.'

"And I said: 'Piggy, I just can't stand to look at that sled any more. I know I can't buy it for Trinket. Some other little girl is going to get it eventually and it breaks my heart.'

"And Pygmalion said: 'The moral of that is—never give up hope!'"

Pygmalion always watched her go with longing for her to stay in his round, black, beady eyes, with loops of gold setting them.

It took her five long breaths to scoot down the

stairs and reach suite 207. To be teaching the princess English seemed to Lucinda the height of absurdity. "I'm only ten, after all," she protested once. "You should get Miss Peters. She could teach arithmetic to a brass monkey."

"But I want you, don't you go for to see?"

"Just—*don't you see,*" corrected Lucinda.

The princess had a lovely way of paying her. At five o'clock, she would take out of her lovely silver chatelaine bag two coins—one big, one small. She would hide these in her hands, hold out the hands, and Lucinda had to choose which one. Sometimes it was the little coin she got—half a dime or ten cents; sometimes it was a quarter or fifty cents. The fifty-cent days troubled Lucinda. It was too, too much for paying a little girl to tell her adored princess what not to say.

So did the Christmas fund grow apace. Lucinda arranged with Vittore to buy the tree on one of his trips to market. She got it for a quarter, very cheap. It stood for three days before Christmas in the corner of the Misses Peters' parlor and made the whole room smell like the spruce woods in Maine after a hot summer rain. It had wide-spreading branches just as she liked them; she hated a spindling tree.

Tony and Miss Nettie helped her make the decorations; Tony coming in after supper, wearing his Sunday clothes and a secret, shy smile that made him look more than ever like the young Michael Angelo. The three made cornucopias out of silver paper, pasted red decalcomanias outside, and hung them with red ribbon to the tree. Out of the scraps left over they rolled long silver icicles. They made paper chains out of tiny links of red and white and silver; and Tony cut stars out of the thin wood of the orange crates and silvered them. Lucinda coaxed Black Sarah into popping corn for clusters. The only ornaments they had to buy for the tree were the candles and tinsel. She stopped half an hour after church the Sunday before to tell Mr. Gideon how wonderful Christmas was turning out, and to thank him again for not passing the plate in her direction. "I expect that's what you'd call tact on your part. I'd like to invite you to the tree, Mr. Gideon, and that isn't tact on my part, it's real appreciation."

Mr. Gideon thanked her and said he might come and then again he might not; it would depend. But he took the Misses Peters' address down very carefully. Lucinda skated home wishing he had made up his mind then and there. If he came she'd have to have a present for him, and if he didn't she'd hate to waste it.

On the afternoon before Christmas, before it was time to go over to Aunt Emily's to be a white tarlatan angel, Lucinda and Miss Nettie made candy to fill the cornucopias. Miss Nettie's candy was almost as good as Louis Sherry's; almost. They made butter toffee and peanut crisp; and some white bonbon stuff out of confectioner's sugar and white of eggs that they rolled into balls and pressed flat between two walnut halves. They didn't crack the shells taking out the meats; and Tony glued them together and silvered them. This last touch made the tree perfectly magnificent.

"It's the nicest tree I ever had, and it will be Trinket's onliest up to now. I do hope you're as excited about it as I am, Miss Nettie." Lucinda spread sugary fingers about Miss Nettie's neck and said something that surprised them both: "I do love you, Miss Nettie."

Eleven sharp, Lucinda had said to all invited. Uncle Earle was to come secretly; all the others openly. She woke Christmas morning with a pop, for all the world like another jack coming out of its box. From the folding bed she could see the tree ready, in the corner, with all the presents on it. After the room was tidied up they would move the tree into the middle so everyone could sit around it—chairs or floor. Would she have to eat a breakfast first? She felt so full of everything else that food—pettyjohn, toast, and cocoa—seemed nonsense. She balanced around that half the tree that stood out from the corner like a sleepy penguin. There was the penwiper she had sewed for Uncle Earle. Wouldn't he boom out like an old cannon at the joke of a Christmas present sewed for him by Lucinda? There were Trinket's red mittens, and Mr. Night Owl's calendar, and everything—everything—everything done up in white paper and tied with red twine.

She had to go and pound on the Misses Peters' bedroom door and shout: "Merry Christmas! Merry Christmas!" And Miss Peters came out and was hugged and discovered to be very hard and bony under her flannelette nightgown; and Miss Nettie came out, with curlers in her hair, and was discovered to be plump and squashy under hers.

At a little before eleven, sharp, two magnificent events occurred. A messenger boy arrived and inquired for Miss Lucinda Wyman. He had a sizable box to deliver with the compliments of Mr. Simon Gideon. It was a box of Louis Sherry's very own candies. To think of Mr. Gideon being so nice! And ten minutes later up the stair puffed Mr. Schultz from the toy-stationery-and-tobacco shop on Eighth Avenue. He puffed because he was carrying the red sled. Lucinda almost sat down with astonishment. To the sled was tied a tag and the tag read:

To Lucinda with a Merry Christmas,
to do with exactly as she likes.
From her friend, Pygmalion.

"I can't wait—I can't wait—I can't wait for eleven

sharp," shouted Lucinda as they moved the tree to the middle of the room and put the red sled under the branches, right where Trinket would see it first as she came in the door. If the tree had looked beautiful upon going to bed it looked now beyond all whooping.

Uncle Earle arrived first. Lucinda was caroling by that time about the wonderful tree that all the children rejoice to see. Uncle Earle flung open the door, his arms full of packages, and Lucinda grabbed him about the middle and they danced like two clumsy bears—a big and a little one. Lucinda shouted: "I rejoice, thou rejoiceth, he, she, and it rejoices! We rejoice, you rejoice, they rejoice! Uncle Earle, I am about to split with rejoicing."

Tony came next. He brought little painted jumping-jacks that he had made to hang on the tree; one for everybody. And a sack full of oranges. "My papa says—Merry Christmas; my mama says—Merry Christmas. I say—Merry Christmas," and he thrust into Lucinda's hand a gift. It was a carved bracelet, leaves and fruit covering the circle and polished with wax to a soft finish. "My papa showed me how they carve frames for the Holy Madonna in Italy. That is how I come to make it."

"It is beautiful, Tony, perfectly beautiful! I shall wear it to every party, and keep it until I die." Lucinda made up her mind on the spot that it would be the greatest treasure she would keep secretly locked inside her desk.

When everyone had arrived and chosen chairs or floor to sit on, Lucinda counted them over to make sure none was missing: The Gilligans, Jerry Hanlon, because he wasn't married, Miss Lucy, honey, Mr. Night Owl, Lady Ross, Aleda Solomon and Buttons, Uncle Earle and Tony, Johanna, from New Jersey, the Misses Peters and herself. Everyone present. Then Uncle Earle and Tony lighted the candles while she scooted up to the third floor and knocked three times on the Browdowskis' door. That was the signal. Then she scooted back again and took her place on the floor beside Tony.

And what do you think! When they came—those three friends—Trinket was holding her mother's hand and Mr. Browdowski—Serge Browdowski, who one day was to become very famous—came with his violin tucked under his chin playing the French carol, "The First Noel." By the time they had reached the wide-flung door all had joined in the singing of it:

"Noel—Noel—Noel—Noel—
Born is the King of Israel."

Not a word spoken, just the singing. It was, as Lucinda whispered to Tony, the loveliest way for Trinket to see her first Christmas tree. She dropped her mother's hand and all alone went around the tree touching with one finger, doll's size, this and that. But the first thing she touched was one of Tony's jumping-jacks. Her tiny mouth was drawn to a pucker and out of it she blew little round "O's" like soap bubbles.

Suddenly she looked about the lighted circle and saw many people. She hunted out Lucinda with her eyes, rushed for her, and buried her face in Lucinda's neck.

The bigger child drew the smaller one down on her lap and then the fun began. Uncle Earle gave out the presents, and what presents they were! Mrs. Gilligan had baked a pound cake for Lucinda; Johanna had made her a pink satin handkerchief case. Mr. Night Owl had brought her Palmer Cox's new Brownie Book. There were dozens of others; besides all of Lucinda's presents for her friends. She had written a verse for everyone, and Uncle Earle read them. The only ones Lucinda ever remembered were the ones that went with Trinket's red mittens and Mr. Gilligan's pipe and tobacco:

> Merry Christmas to Trinket,
>   These red mittens say.
> We'll keep warm her hands
>   When she goes out to play.

And to Mr. Gilligan:

> 'Tis a grand thing to be Irish,
>   And to have an Irish pipe.
> May it never need a filling,
>   May it never need a light.

Lucinda explained that she knew pipe and light didn't rhyme very well but she hoped Mr. Gilligan wouldn't mind.

There is always one Christmas that belongs to you more than any other—belongs by right of festival and those secret feelings that are never spoken aloud. This Christmas belonged to Lucinda in this way, and I think it belonged to many of her friends. I know it was the only

Christmas the Browdowskis kept everlastingly green in their hearts.

As the party was breaking up—Mr. Gilligan having to get back to his fares—Uncle Earle put thumb and forefinger into his breast pocket rumbling out something about forgetting. "Always carry these with me for the children at Christmas. Just got three left!" And into the pocket of Lucinda's best pinafore, into a pocket of Tony's Sunday clothes, and into one of Trinket's red Christmas mittens went a gold piece.

"Bless me, don't thank me," said Uncle Earle. "I just go down to the bank the day before Christmas and ask for a pocketful to give away. And they're always nice about it."

As a party it had Aunt Emily's beaten hollow, so Lucinda told Miss Nettie. Miss Peters let Lucinda keep the tree until Twelfth Night, and every day until January sixth, Trinket came down at dusk, and she and Lucinda watched the burning candles, and talked softly together about the first time Trinket had seen it. "Long as we live, Trinket, we'll remember this Christmas—a four-year-old Christmas for you and a ten-year-old Christmas for me."

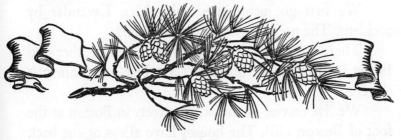

Christmas in the Street of Memories
An Adventure in Boston

Elizabeth Rhodes Jackson

The Prince and Princess lived with Mr. Lifsky on the street floor, and we live on the next floor, and old Mrs. Lavendar lives on the top floor.

We first got acquainted with Mrs. Lavendar by accident. The accident happened to Beany.

There are three of us. Jack is my older brother and Beany is my younger brother. I am Dee and I am just eleven.

We live on one of the oldest streets in Boston at the foot of Beacon Hill. The houses have alleys at the back or through their cellars, and we play tag in them. The alleys all run into each other and make a sort of maze. You run up an alley and climb over a couple of fences and down another alley and through a gate and there you are in another street. We were all playing one day after school, and Beany went to climb a fence and fell, right on his face. Beany would, you know. He's always the one of us that has the falls. He bruised his forehead and skinned his nose. He was very brave about it and didn't cry, although the tears were in his eyes.

We took him home, Jack and I, but when we took Beany upstairs to our landing, the door was locked and Mother was out. Beany had been brave so long that he couldn't wait any longer, and while I was fumbling in the regular place for the key, he burst out into a long, sad wail. Then a lady on the floor above, who was a stranger to us, leaned over the banister and said, "Bring him up to me."

Her apartment was very lovely with beautiful old furniture and soft, thick rugs on the floor and huge silver candlesticks on the mantel. But there was no fire in the fireplace, though the day was cold, and she had on a beautiful white silk shawl with an embroidered border. She took Beany on her lap and washed the dirt off his face very gently. Then she held him in her arms and we sat on the rug, and she told us about her son when he was a little boy.

That was how we got acquainted with Mrs. Lavendar. And that was the way we came to find the Prince and the Princess.

Mother calls the street we live on the Street of Memories for two reasons. One is that memories of the past are still living there. Two blocks from our house, at the corner of Boston Common, is the spot where the British soldiers embarked the night that Paul Revere got ahead of them on his famous ride. Two blocks the other way Oliver Wendell Holmes used to live. And Miss Alcott walked on our street many and many a time. I love to walk up the hill to see the little brick house where she and her sister kept house—Jo and Amy— in their struggling days, and on the way home I pass the stately mansion (Dr. Holmes said that in "The Chambered Nautilus"), where she lived when she was successful and famous.

The other reason Mother calls it the Street of Memories is because of the antique shops all up and down the street. Some of them are very artistic, with nothing but two colonial chairs and a table in the window. But we like best the ones that have the windows crowded full of new and interesting things. Mr. Lifsky's is like that, on the street floor of our house. His show window is just jammed with three ship models and some colored bottles, and a battered old lantern, and andirons and silhouettes in tiny frames and an inlaid snuff box and a pair of china dogs and a luster tea set, and hanging up are old engravings and faded samplers.

We were all three looking into Mr. Lifsky's window one day when Mrs. Lavendar came out and saw us there. We knew her very well by that time.

"Mrs. Lavendar, do see this ship's model," said Jack.

"It looks like all sorts of adventures," she said, and then she caught her breath a little.

"How long have those been here?" she said. "I haven't seen them before."

She was pointing to a pair of china figures, a lady and gentleman in elaborate old-fashioned dress. The lady had wide skirts and high powdered hair and flowers on her breast, and the gentleman had a ruffled shirt and knee breeches and buckled shoes. They were tiny but very perfect and delicate, and the faces were exquisitely beautiful.

"I'm sure those are mine," said Mrs. Lavendar very low. Then she walked into Mr. Lifsky's shop.

"She's going in to buy them," we said, but presently she came out without them.

We told Mother about it. "Why do you think she didn't buy them?" asked Jack.

"Probably Mr. Lifsky's price was too high," said Mother.

"Oh, but Mrs. Lavendar is rich," said Beany. "You ought to see her beautiful apartment."

"I'm afraid not," said Mother. "She used to have a great deal of money, but now she is old and poor and alone. Her son gave up his life in the war, you know."

"I wonder if that is why she doesn't have a fire in the fireplace," I said, for we often went up to see her now, and her apartment was usually cold. Of course, the house is supposed to be heated from the cellar, but we always have two log fires going in winter to help out. Our house is a beautiful old residence that has been made over into apartments, so the plumbing and heating are old-fashioned and often cause us trouble.

A week later we had cold weather. Cold weather in Boston is *very* cold. I don't believe even the North Pole is any colder than the Street of Memories in winter!

"I was going to suggest your going up to see Mrs. Lavendar," said Mother, when we came home from school, "but it is so cold, perhaps you'd better take a fire with you."

I followed her up the stairs and heard her saying, "Mrs. Lavendar, would it bother you if the children made a little call?"

"I'd love to have them," said Mrs. Lavendar, "only I'm afraid the room is rather cold. I can't seem to get enough heat."

"It's a frightful heating system, isn't it?" said Mother. "We've had to have a hearthfire today. Jack will bring up some wood, if you don't mind the litter."

So soon we were on the way up, Jack with a basket of logs and Beany carrying the paper bag of kindling and I with the hearth brush. Beany, poor child, tripped over the rug and dropped the bag, which split open, but Mrs. Lavendar was very nice about it, and I swept up the debris and it was all right. Jack made a glorious fire and we were very cozy. Knowing Mother, I suspect she planned the whole thing just to get Mrs. Lavendar warm.

While we were all sitting there as happy as could be, Beany suddenly spoke up. Beany too frequently says things he shouldn't, and what he said this time was, "Mrs. Lavendar, how did your china figures come to be in Mr. Lifsky's antique shop?"

We tried to hush him, but Mrs. Lavendar said, "I sold all the furnishings of my house some years ago, except what I have here, and the little Prince and Princess went with the rest."

"Are they a Prince and Princess?" I asked.

"That was the name my boy had for them when he was little." And somehow, from the way she said it, I knew that she missed the little china figures.

Then Beany piped up again. "Why did you have to sell your furniture, Mrs. Lavendar, when you have so much money?"

We couldn't hush him at all, but Mrs. Lavendar understood and she only smiled and said, "I haven't much money, dear. I had some, but it was taken from me. So I had to sell the furniture to get money to live on."

"How was it taken?" said Beany, all interest.

"It isn't a very pleasant story," said Mrs. Lavendar. "My investments were in a business that could not go on until the war was over."

Beany nodded, though he didn't understand. We did partly.

"My son's salary was enough for us till he went to war. Then we planned to sell our house and invest the money to take care of me till he came back."

"I see," said Beany.

"My son came in with the money from the sale one afternoon. He wouldn't take a check because sometimes checks can't be collected. He went to the bank with the man who bought the house, and the man drew the money in bills and gave it to him—forty thousand dollars. It was too late to take the money to my bank for deposit that day, so he brought it home to me, and it was taken that same day."

"Who took it?" we said together.

"I never knew," said Mrs. Lavendar. "Not the servants. They had been with me for years. Someone must have come in—but I don't know how. It has always been a mystery."

"Where was it?" we asked.

"In the Governor Winthrop desk," said old Mrs. Lavendar. "That very desk there against the wall. My son said, 'I'll put it in here, Mother.' I saw him with his hand on the open leaf of the desk. I said, 'Yes, that's a perfectly safe place.' I went out to see my son off then, and I was so confused and troubled over parting with him, that I forgot to lock it. And when I went to get the money next day to take it to the bank, it was not there."

"This very desk!" said Jack. We were all very much excited, for we knew that some of those old desks have secret drawers and false backs to the pigeon-holes. It seemed perfectly clear to us that there were forty thousand dollars somewhere inside that solid square old piece of mahogany, and if we could find it, Mrs. Lavendar would be rich again. We told her so very excitedly, but she shook her head.

"I've known this desk all my life, dear," she said. "It was my great-grandfather's. I know every nook and corner of it. It has no secrets."

"May we look through it?" we said. "We might be able to find *something*."

Of course, Mrs. Lavendar let us, and we took out all the papers and the drawers, and measured and tapped and pushed to find secret springs. But we had to give it up at last. If the money was still there, hidden in some secret place, it was too successfully hidden for us to find.

I noticed that the beautiful silver candlesticks were not on the mantel, and Mrs. Lavendar was wearing a little black sweater instead of the embroidered shawl. I was afraid Beany would notice and ask if she had to sell them, too, but he was too interested in the desk to ask questions about anything else.

For several days we talked about the money and then we forgot all about it for a while, because of Christmas. We were busy as could be, writing our Christmas wants and making things and counting our savings and going shopping for presents after school. We all painted cards for Mrs. Lavendar, of course, and it was while we were doing this, one snowy day, that I said, "Oh, dear, I wish we could buy the Prince and Princess and give them to Mrs. Lavendar for Christmas!"

"That's just like you, Dee," said Jack. "One of those brilliant ideas that there's no way of carrying out!"

I knew he didn't mean that to sound unpleasant. It was just that he wanted so much to do it, and didn't see how we could.

"Let's ask Mr. Lifsky how much they are, anyway!" said Beany.

Beany is always so hopeful. Jack and I knew it was useless, because we had already spent all our money for Christmas. But Beany went down to ask Mr. Lifsky and came back soon to tell us.

"Seven dollars and fifty cents." He said it just as cheerfully as if we had seven dollars and fifty cents right there.

And then something very unexpected happened. We were playing tag in the back alley a few days later and by mistake we tipped over an ash barrel. When we went to pick up the junk we had spilled, we found some old bundles of letters tied with faded ribbon and photographs and some good camera films. Someone had just moved out of the house, and there was no one there but

a cleaning woman. We showed her the films and asked
if we could have them, and she said we could have anything we found in the back yard, but we must clean up
any rubbish we spilled. There were four or five barrels
in the yard and we dumped them all out, one after another, and found a number of very worth while articles.
But the really important thing was two filled books of
trading stamps, and when we saw those, we knew, after
all, that there was hope of our buying the Prince and
Princess.

We took the stamps home to Mother and she said they were worth two dollars for each book and that it would be all right for Jack to go and get the money for them, as otherwise they would be burned for rubbish. So while Jack hurried off across the Common to the department stores, Beany and I went back to dig again for buried treasure. We didn't find anything else in the barrels, but Beany spied a row of store milk bottles, and we gathered those up and took them back to the chain store. There were twenty-one of them, and that gave us a dollar and five cents, so when Jack came back with the trading stamp money, we had five dollars and five cents altogether.

"Perhaps Mr. Lifsky would come down," said Jack. "People always do bargain for antiques, you know."

So we took the five one-dollar bills and the nickel and showed them to Mr. Lifsky. We told him that was all the money we had and asked if he would sell us the pair of china figures. We couldn't pay another cent for them.

"For fife tollars und fife cents you ask it!" said Mr. Lifsky indignantly. "Ten times ofer could I sell them little fickures for fife tollars und fife cents! Seven-fifty ist mine brice, und not one cent less than fife-fifty."

"We haven't got five-fifty," said Jack.

"Fife-fifty!" Mr. Lifsky said again, so we went out to talk it over.

"We almost have it," said Jack. "Only forty-five cents. Let's all think hard."

So we all thought hard. But it was Beany who thought of asking Mother to advance forty-five cents of our pocket money. There was a great shout of joy from us all when he came back with it. We went right in to Mr. Lifsky's and bought the Prince and Princess. They were a little bit dusty, and Jack thought we ought to put them into the bathtub and wash them. But Mother thought not, because we might chip them or wash off the color, and Mrs. Lavendar would know best how to clean them. Then we started to wrap them in Christmas paper, but we were afraid that Mrs. Lavendar might break them in opening them. Besides it would be more fun to have her see them right away, the minute she opened the door.

Jack wanted to be the one to carry the Prince and I wanted to carry the Princess, and Beany felt very bad about it.

"It's just because I'm the youngest," he said. "I have to take turns with you filling the wood-basket and going to the store, but no one ever takes turns with me being the youngest. I thought how to get the last forty-five cents, anyway. And Mrs. Lavendar was my friend first."

So we told him he could be the one to say, "Merry Christmas, Mrs. Lavendar; we've brought you a present." So it was settled.

Christmas Eve is very beautiful on Beacon Hill. All the houses are lighted with candles in every window, and the curtains are drawn back so that everyone can see the inside. The houses are all very beautiful to see, too, because most of them were built in early days and have winding staircases and paneled walls, and many of them have beautiful tapestries and paintings. A great crowd comes from all over Boston, so that you can hardly move through the streets, but everyone is quiet and reverent. It is almost like church outdoors, especially after the carols begin. Mother always takes us out for a little while, after we have lighted the candles in our own windows.

This Christmas Eve we asked Mrs. Lavendar to go out with us, but she thought she might get too tired. So when we came back, we three sang carols just for her—"Silent Night, Holy Night" and "The First Noel"—looking up at the candles in her windows.

It is such an exciting feeling to wake on Christmas morning and see the stockings all humpy. But this Christmas I had a specially joyous feeling, and I remembered we were going to take the Prince and Princess to Mrs. Lavendar.

Right after breakfast we went upstairs, Jack carrying the Prince and I carrying the Princess, just as we had planned. But halfway upstairs I caught a glimpse of Beany's face. He had a scratch across his chin where the grocer's cat had scratched him, when he tried to pet her, and he had such a sad look that I was sorry for him. It must be hard to be the youngest. So I said, "Here, Beany, you can carry her," and handed him the Princess.

We got to the top of the stairs and Jack looked around and saw how it was, and he said, "Oh, well," and he put the Prince into my hands. So after all it was Jack who lifted the brass knocker and said, "Merry Christmas, Mrs. Lavendar; we've brought you a present."

But when she saw the Prince and Princess, she said, "Oh, you dear children!" very softly.

Then she said, "Their home is on the desk, dears, one on each side of my son's picture." I walked across the room and put the Prince on the desk very carefully, and Beany came next.

But then Beany slipped and down he came—crash! —on the floor. Beany *would!*

Mrs. Lavendar stooped over the pieces.

"I am sure we can mend the Princess," she was saying and then she gasped and picked up something from under the pieces.

It was a roll of bills that had been inside the hollow Princess.

"The money was not taken," she said slowly. "It was there all the time."

She sat down and her hands were trembling.

"I begin to understand," she said. "My son was standing by the desk. I never thought of the Princess. But of course he would put it there. From the time he was a baby he used to stow all sorts of little treasures through that hole in the base. He thought of course that I saw him putting it there and that no one else would know."

We had a great rejoicing after that, and since then

Mrs. Lavendar hasn't gone out to do sewing any more. The silver candlesticks are back on the mantel and she wears the white silk shawl and has a fire, too, on cold days. And she has mended the Princess with china cement so you can't see the cracks at all unless you get up very close.

THE MAGIC OF CHRISTMAS

Pegasus and the Star

John Brangwyn

Somebody was blowing bubbles, and one of them had drifted to the meadow where Pegasus, the winged horse, had his home. He leaped into the air. Fortunately he had learned to move very gently, for if he had beat the air with quick strokes of those beautiful wings the bubble would have burst and Pegasus would never have had the adventure.

He got as close as he could to the dazzling globe and when he was nearer he could see a picture painted on it in all those colors which bubbles use. He held his breath and flew softly. But as the picture turned and turned whenever the bubble did, he had hard work making it out.

The picture was of a room in an old house where the rafters showed in the ceiling; there was a wood fire on the hearth and two lighted candles on the mantelpiece. Grandfather sat on one side of the fireplace, holding his cane between his knees, and Grandmother sat on the other with a snowy white cap on her head.

"Please don't get so near," said the bubble. "I don't want to burst just yet, for I still have a long way to go."

Pegasus was so glad to hear the bubble speak that he almost snorted with pleasure, which would have put an end to the story. But he caught his breath in time and asked in a whisper, "Where are you going?"

"I don't really know," replied the bubble. "Perhaps around the world."

Pegasus wished that he could go along, but it did not seem polite to ask, so he said, "That's a beautiful picture you have painted on you, but I wish you could hold still just a minute so that I can see if that tree is in the room or outside."

"I can't stop even a minute," said the bubble, "but I can tell you that the tree is in the room."

"That's queer!" said Pegasus. "The woodcutter always cuts up the tree before he takes it in."

Then he edged up a little nearer and looked more closely. "What queer fruit that tree has," he said.

The bubble laughed merrily, as only bubbles can, and rolled over and over so fast that the picture was entirely blurred and you would have said it was part of the rainbow rolled up in a ball.

"That isn't fruit," said the bubble. "That's the Christmas trimming, candles and tinsel paper and toys and all sorts of things."

"What for?" asked Pegasus, just to say something because all these words were new ones to him.

"For Christmas," said the bubble.

Pegasus began to be very impatient; it was bad enough to have to fly so carefully that he was beginning to get fidgety in his feathers, but to listen to so many things that he could not understand—that was too much!

The bubble liked to talk, and so it went on: "When the candles are lighted everything on the tree will glitter and the children will sing their songs and the old people will talk about the weather and about old days and everyone will say, 'Merry Christmas,' a great many times."

"I'd like to be there!" said Pegasus softly.

"With your wings," replied the bubble admiringly, "you can get there before the candles are lighted."

"What direction do I take?" asked Pegasus, fairly on tiptoe with excitement.

"Keep the North Wind in your face," said the bubble. "You'll see the village on a hillside; it looks just like a Christmas card."

"I've never seen a Christmas card," said Pegasus, quite embarrassed.

"Well," said the bubble, "the church spire will be the highest point in the picture, and there are usually two or three people going up the hill to church. And then there are some little houses with lights in their

windows, and some children outside one of them singing carols, and a forest in the background with snow on
the branches of all the trees. But you'll have to come
down to earth to get into the village because the streets
aren't wide enough for your wings."

That made Pegasus pause. He never felt quite safe
when his wings were too tightly folded; it made getting
away so much harder. But perhaps the streets were paved
with cobblestones.

The bubble said they were, and wanted to know
what difference that made.

"If I can strike sparks with my flinty hoofs," said
Pegasus, "I can frighten them."

"That is *not* the spirit to go in," said the bubble,
acting very indignant.

"I wouldn't go in that spirit," replied Pegasus, "but
if there was any danger I might have to leave in it."

"Good luck to you," said the bubble and sailed off
into the sky, "exactly as though it had wings," thought
Pegasus to himself.

Without wasting a minute Pegasus turned himself
about until he felt the North Wind in his nostrils. He
liked it the least of the four winds, but, if that was the
only way to find the village and the tree *in* the house,
he would take it.

He flew and he flew over countries he had never
seen before. For deep in his heart Pegasus was a home-
body and never left his meadow for too long flights. But
today he was urged on by a desire so strong that he did
not feel at all afraid. He would have liked to stop and

visit some of the places he was flying over, but that might make him too late to see the tree lighted, and so he hurried on.

The North Wind got colder and colder; it whistled in his ears to discourage him; it changed the falling rain into icy sleet, the first that Pegasus had ever seen or felt. His long, curly eyelashes were frozen stiff, and he began to feel his wings growing heavy with it. And to see his own breath turn into icicles was terrifying!

He was over a deep wood when this happened and he dared not go too near the earth, although it might be warmer down there. He had once been lost in a wood and he had never forgotten it. He peered through the dusk for a road, for if he could run upon the earth he could warm himself up and shake this ice off his wings. But there was no road, and suddenly he could not believe his eyes: the world was turning white! The rain and sleet itself had turned into little white feathers which melted when they touched his soft nose. The branches of the trees were soon covered with them, and then he knew he must be somewhere near the village.

Only one fear hovered about him now—that it might be too dark to see the church spire and the little houses. This fear began to grow and grow until it was bigger and darker than any of the shadows in the forest. And just as it was going to rob him of strength to go on and bring him crashing down into the wood, he heard a bell ringing a little way off to his right.

Now you have heard church bells all your life but this was the first one Pegasus had ever heard. It seemed to him the most wonderful music in the world—as it is.

He flew straight towards it, happy as a lark. And he saw the spire and the church and two or three people going up the hill to it. He saw the houses with lights in the windows and the children singing in front of one of them. Their voices were like the purest of bells.

Then he remembered about the street being narrow and so he flew down gently at the very edge of town. The children who saw him floating down through the snowflakes believed more than ever in the story of the Snow Queen, for here was one of her horses as white and as light as snow, trotting along their own village street!

They had been a bit afraid to come very near him, and they were really much relieved when they were called into supper. Their parents smiled when they told of what they had seen and they were not scolded for exaggerating, because it was Christmas Eve and children were so imaginative.

Pegasus heard such a clatter! And to his dismay all

the shutters were being closed before he had even found
the house with the tree in it. Only the baker's door was
open, and there was no tree there. But oh, how warm and
comfortable it looked! He would have liked to go in, but
the baker shut the door in his face with a bang. Now
Pegasus wondered if he had come so far to stand, cold
and hungry, outside a bakeshop.

It had stopped snowing and the moon, looking very
much like the bubble, shone gloriously upon the church
spire and on the white roofs of the houses. Here and
there Pegasus could see a red glow coming out from
under a door or from between two shutters and he could
hear all sorts of strange noises which might be the way
candles sounded when they were being lighted, Pegasus
thought.

What could he do? He ought to have thought of
this before he started and have asked the bubble how to
act after he had found the village. Perhaps he ought not
to have come at all! If he had frightened the children
and even the baker, who had turned pale under his flour,
how could he expect to find anyone who would ask him
in?

He wandered back to the bakeshop window where
the shutters were not up so that everyone could see the
bread and cakes and the gingerbread men and animals.
The frost was beginning to draw designs all over the
glass. Pegasus had never seen frost before and he almost
forgot his discomfort in watching the ferns and flowers
grow under his gaze and the rivers and woods, just as
he had seen them during his flight.

The baker's wife had noticed the frost, too. "It is

getting colder," she said, and went to the window to move the gingerbread men where they would not get wet when it melted.

And there stood Pegasus, his beautiful eyes looking in from the street, his creamy white mane blowing about his head in the moonlight. She looked him straight in the eyes and she was not frightened. But he dared not move for fear she would go away. Only he had to take a long breath, and it turned into steaming white plumes all about his head.

The baker's wife moved first. She came quickly to the door with a piece of hot gingerbread just out of the oven. "Are you hungry?" she asked.

"Terribly," said Pegasus, and she gave him the gingerbread loaf which he ate in two mouthfuls.

"You must be cold, too," she said, "although you have a blanket folded upon your back."

Pegasus did not tell her that it was his wings, for wings, he had learned, frighten so many people.

"I wouldn't be cold if I weren't so dripping wet," he said.

"There's room in our stable," she said invitingly, "with warm straw and an extra blanket."

Now Pegasus had never been in a stable, nor had he ever felt the need of warm straw, but he nodded to show his gratitude for her kindness. The baker's wife threw a cape over her shoulders, closed the door carefully behind her, and showed him the way to the stable behind the house.

It was a dark place even when she had lighted the

lantern, and it did not feel at all warm, but Pegasus did not want to complain.

The baker's wife threw straw on the floor of the stall and put some sweet-smelling hay in the manger, and then she lifted the lantern to see what sort of blanket he was wearing. Just then Pegasus shivered and his wings opened just a little in spite of him. The baker's wife gave a shriek and dropped the lantern which, fortunately, went out, or it might have set the straw on fire.

But curiosity got the better of the kind woman, and she soon came back with her husband, carrying a bigger lantern.

"Please do not be afraid of me," said Pegasus as he saw them in the doorway. "I came a long way to see the candles lighted on a tree *inside* a house where Grandfather and Grandmother are sitting by the fireplace."

He had said it all at once and as quickly as possible, for it had to be heard! It was.

"What is that on your back?" asked the baker's wife.

"My wings," said Pegasus sadly, "and they are very wet."

"Poor dear!" said the baker's wife, and sent her husband for a comforter to put over the blanket she had brought.

"Wings," she said, all excitement. "So you are an angel, a Christmas angel, disguised as a horse."

Pegasus began to feel very happy and important. "If I could only see the candles lighted," he said, bending his lovely neck in an appealing way.

"But the room wouldn't hold you and the tree at the same time," she said, "even if you could get in any door in the village, which you couldn't."

But she stroked his silky mane. "Could you make yourself smaller?" she asked.

"I can't change myself at all," said Pegasus.

"I could put a spell on you," said the baker's wife, brightening up and taking the thick comforter from her husband and sending him back for two lumps of sugar.

"Is this a spell?" asked Pegasus, eyeing the quilt.

She did not answer directly. "Suppose I turn you into a gingerbread horse and hang you up on the tree where you could see everything. Would you like that?"

Pegasus remembered how he had gobbled down the gingerbread. "Mightn't somebody eat me?" he asked, a little fearful.

"I'll put thick white frosting on and they won't let the children eat you tonight because you are too sweet. And tomorrow morning I will take the spell off."

It was very strange how sleepy he got as he stood there in the stable, waiting for the spell, and wondering how it would look, and feeling just a little worried. Would he have come if he had known about it and about the shutters being closed; would he?

But it was too late to bother about anything, for there he was hanging up on the fir tree, not far from the silver star. He could feel that the frosting was not quite dry, but it was so much drier than he had been out

there in the stable that he felt quite comfortable. Besides, ginger itself is warming.

It was more beautiful here than he had dreamed. The firelight and the two candles on the mantelpiece made dancing shadows all over the room. Grandfather and Grandmother were not sitting down, as in the bubble's picture, but were very busy filling small packages, putting red apples into one dish and cakes into another. And the slender white candles in their bright tin holders were full of promise.

Grandfather stood up on a stool to light them. Grandmother held the stool and was very much worried that he'd fall off, or that he'd set the tree on fire, or that the tree was not as gay as last year.

"But last year," said Grandfather, "we did not have a winged horse."

"The baker's wife is full of good ideas," said Grandmother, "but I am not sure that she uses good butter."

The candles were all lighted. One of them was a little too near Pegasus for comfort, but it would do no harm to get toasted after such a soaking as he had had. Full of contentment he looked and listened. Everything was ready; the chestnuts were popping on the hearth, and the candles were shining like golden stars. The hubbub just outside the door was the only thing that Pegasus could not understand. He had never heard anything like it!

Neither had the old people either, they said, when they had opened the door and let in the children with their parents. They came in red hoods and mittens; they hugged and kissed Grandfather and Grandmother, and danced around the tree, as much surprised by it as was Pegasus himself, who had never been to a children's party before. He watched the little packages being opened and smelled the toasting chestnuts and the cider; and he almost lost his balance trying to see it all at once with his little brown-sugar eyes.

But the most exciting moment for Pegasus was when the children discovered him near the silver star. "A white horse with wings!" they cried. "Where did you get it, Grandfather?"

"The baker's wife brought it in just before we lighted the tree," he replied.

"Then it's nothing but gingerbread and frosting," said the oldest little boy, disappointed.

"Oh, let me have him to eat!" cried the smallest little girl, holding out her hands.

Pegasus began to tremble so much that the frosting got crinkled and he was glad to hear Grandfather say, "Not tonight. You have had enough sweets." The baker's wife was a wise woman, after all.

Then the children sat down on the floor and began to sing. Pegasus had never heard music like it; it made the raftered room change into a hilltop where shepherds were looking up at a star and listening to angelic voices. Then the music turned that silent hilltop into a stable, very much like the one Pegasus had just been in; and the angelic voices sang on, and the silver star shone into the open door.

And there, where a moment before Grandfather and Grandmother had been sitting, was the manger full of sweet hay and, lying upon a blanket of white wool, was a Child, smaller and more beautiful than any of the children whose voices seemed now to be coming out of the starry sky. The Child was smiling; all about Him was the glow of unseen candles, and in their light Pegasus saw the little gray ass and the sheep looking, just as he was looking in wonder and praise.

Then in came the Three Kings, and when they kneeled down to make their gifts, the frankincense was burning, and Pegasus could get its smell as its smoke blurred the scene before him.

Now he knew why he had come so far and been made little enough to see the candles lighted upon the tree. When the singing was over he kept his eyes closed to recall what he had just seen. But he could hear the children talking and the fire spluttering, and suddenly he felt a warm little hand untying the ribbon which held him in place. He opened his eyes and his heart nearly stopped beating! He wanted to cry out, but his throat was dry; it was the smallest little girl who had climbed up on a stool when Grandfather was not looking. Very carefully she climbed down again with Pegasus in her hand. She looked into his brown-sugar eyes and he looked back appealingly. It was impossible to tell whether admiration or hunger was shining in the blue depths.

Then she held him close to her flushed little face— for she knew she was being disobedient—and she licked the frosting upon his wings. It was just as he had feared; he was going to be eaten!

But suddenly, before her sharp little white teeth could bite into him, the door opened and a man put his head into the room.

"The baker's house is on fire," he said.

What a pell-mell rushing there was then! Grandfather dropped his cane and grabbed the water bucket by the door; the children ran out without putting on their caps. Only Grandmother stayed behind a moment to put her white cap in the top bureau drawer, and to blow out the candles.

The little girl with Pegasus in her hand was running, too, trying to keep up with the others. When she got to the baker's shop she began to cry and kept as close as she could to her mother. But no one paid any attention to her, and she squeezed poor Pegasus so that he almost fainted. He could hear, however, the men calling for more pails.

"Oh!" cried the baker's wife. "If we could only get the Mayor's water cart!"

"But we can't spare anyone to go for it, and the Mayor has gone to town with his horse," said Grandfather.

"There's a strange horse in the baker's stable," called out a boy who came running around the corner of the house. "Let me harness him and go for the water cart!"

And back he went without waiting for permission, while the men passed the buckets as fast as they could, and the women helped the baker's wife get out her bedroom furniture.

Then the boy came running back, his eyes big with fear. "It's a dead horse and it has wings!" he cried.

The baker's wife heard him. "It's not dead," she called. "Run to the Christmas tree and bring me the frosted horse under the silver star." And the boy ran off.

Then the little girl could stand it no longer. She ran to the baker's wife and held out the frosted horse. "Here it is," she said. "I didn't eat him."

The baker's wife seized the cake and ran into the stable, and in another minute Pegasus felt someone putting harness on him. It was the first time in his life that harness had ever touched him. But he stood quite still and kept his wings folded. Then he leaped off up the hill, dragging the boy so fast at the end of the reins that his feet never touched the ground till he got to the Mayor's.

The boy hitched Pegasus to the water cart and back they went. It had taken less than three minutes, and there was enough water now to put out the fire. Pegasus felt full of comfort that he had been able so quickly to repay the baker's wife for giving him the chance to see why the candles were lit at Christmas on a tree, brought in from the woods and set up in the house. But he did not want to talk about it, and so he wandered off to the stable and looked in. The lantern was still hanging by the stall; a soft glow came from the manger and the scent of hay, and he thought that he could still hear the voices in the sky. He kneeled down for a moment and then, slipping out of his harness, he unfolded his wings and mounted straight to the silver stars and turned to find the South Wind in his nostrils.

He could see the church spire and the little houses. The lights were in the windows because everyone had thrown open the shutters to look at the fire in the baker's shop. The fire was out now and everyone was amazed to find that it had done no harm at all!

Pegasus flew through the night and did not stop until he had reached the cedar in his meadow, and told it all that had happened.

"But why are you looking at me so queerly?" asked the cedar.

"I am looking to see where we can put the candles next Christmas," said Pegasus.

The Christmas Masquerade

Mary E. Wilkins Freeman

On Christmas Eve the Mayor's stately mansion presented a beautiful appearance. There were rows of different colored wax candles burning in every window,
and beyond them one could see the chandeliers of gold
and crystal blazing with light. The fiddles were squeak-
ing merrily, and lovely little forms flew past the windows in time to the music.

There were gorgeous carpets laid from the door to
the street, and carriages were constantly arriving and
fresh guests tripping over them. They were all children.
The Mayor was giving a Christmas Masquerade tonight
to all the children in the city, the poor as well as the rich.

The preparation for this ball had been making an immense sensation for the last three months. Placards had been up in the most conspicuous points in the city, and all the daily newspapers had at least a column devoted to it, headed with THE MAYOR'S CHRISTMAS MASQUERADE in very large letters.

The Mayor had promised to defray the expenses of all the poor children whose parents were unable to do so, and the bills for their costumes were directed to be sent in to him.

Of course there was great excitement among the regular costumers of the city, and they all resolved to vie with one another in being the most popular, and the best patronized on this gala occasion. But the placards and the notices had not been out a week before a new Costumer appeared who cast all the others into the shade directly. He set up his shop on the corner of one of the principal streets, and hung up his beautiful costumes in the windows. He was a little fellow, not much larger than a boy of ten. His cheeks were as red as roses, and he had on a long curling wig as white as snow. He wore a suit of crimson velvet knee breeches, and a little swallow-tailed coat with beautiful golden buttons. Deep lace ruffles fell over his slender white hands, and he wore elegant knee buckles of glittering stones. He sat on a high stool behind his counter and served his customers himself; he kept no clerk.

It did not take the children long to discover what beautiful things he had, and how superior he was to the other costumers, and they began to flock to his shop immediately, from the Mayor's daughter to the poor ragpicker's. The children were to select their own costumes; the Mayor had stipulated that. It was to be a children's ball in every sense of the word.

So they decided to be fairies, and shepherdesses, and princesses, according to their own fancies; and this new Costumer had charming costumes to suit them.

It was noticeable that, for the most part, the children of the rich, who had always had everything they desired, would choose the parts of goose-girls and peasants and such like; and the poor children jumped eagerly at the chance of being princesses or fairies for a few hours in their miserable lives.

When Christmas Eve came and the children flocked into the Mayor's mansion, whether it was owing to the Costumer's art, or their own adaptation to the characters they had chosen, it was wonderful how lifelike their representations were. Those little fairies in their short skirts of silken gauze, in which golden sparkles appeared as they moved, with their little funny gossamer wings, like butterflies, looked like real fairies. It did not seem possible, when they floated around to the music, half supported on the tips of their dainty toes, half by their filmy purple wings, their delicate bodies swaying in time, that they could be anything but fairies. It seemed absurd to imagine that they were Johnny Mullens, the washerwoman's son, and Polly Flinders, the charwoman's little girl, and so on.

The Mayor's daughter, who had chosen the character of a goose-girl, looked so like a true one that one could hardly dream she ever was anything else. She was, ordinarily, a slender, dainty little lady rather tall for her age. She now looked very short and stubbed and brown, just as if she had been accustomed to tend geese in all sorts of weather. It was so with all the others—the Red Riding-hoods, the princesses, the Bo-Peeps, and with every one of the characters who came to the Mayor's ball; Red Riding-hood looked round, with big, frightened eyes, all ready to spy the wolf, and carried her little pat of butter and pot of honey gingerly in her basket; Bo-Peep's eyes looked red with weeping for the loss of her sheep; and the princesses swept about so grandly in their splendid brocaded trains, and held their crowned heads so high that people half-believed them to be true princesses.

But there never was anything like the fun at the Mayor's Christmas ball. The fiddlers fiddled and fiddled, and the children danced and danced on the beautiful waxed floors. The Mayor, with his family and a few grand guests, sat on a dais covered with blue velvet at one end of the dancing hall, and watched the sport. They were all delighted. The Mayor's eldest daughter sat in front and clapped her little soft white hands. She was a tall, beautiful young maiden, and wore a white dress, and a little cap woven of blue violets on her yellow hair. Her name was Violetta.

The supper was served at midnight—and such a supper! The mountains of pink and white ices, and the cakes with sugar castles and flower gardens on the tops of them, and the charming shapes of gold and ruby-colored jellies. There were wonderful bonbons which even the Mayor's daughter did not have every day; and all

sorts of fruits, fresh and candied. . . . Under each child's plate there was a pretty present and every one had a basket of bonbons and cake to carry home.

At four o'clock the fiddlers put up their fiddles and the children went home; fairies and shepherdesses and pages and princesses all jabbering gleefully about the splendid time they had had.

But in a short time what consternation there was throughout the city! When the proud and fond parents attempted to unbutton their children's dresses, in order to prepare them for bed, not a single costume would come off. The buttons buttoned again as fast as they were unbuttoned; even if they pulled out a pin, in it would slip again in a twinkling; and when a string was untied it tied itself up again into a bowknot. The parents were dreadfully frightened. But the children were so tired out they finally let them go to bed in their fancy costumes and thought perhaps they would come off better in the morning. So Red Riding-hood went to bed in her little red cloak, holding fast to her basket full of dainties for her grandmother, and Bo-Peep slept with her crook in her hand.

The children all went to bed readily enough, they were so very tired, even though they had to go in this strange array. All but the fairies—they danced and pirouetted and would not be still.

"We want to swing on the blades of grass," they kept saying, "and play hide and seek in the lily cups, and take a nap between the leaves of the roses."

The poor charwomen and coal-heavers, whose children the fairies were for the most part, stared at them in great distress. They did not know what to do with these radiant, frisky little creatures into which their Johnnys and their Pollys and Betseys were so suddenly transformed. But the fairies went to bed quietly enough when daylight came, and were soon fast asleep.

There was no further trouble till twelve o'clock, when all the children woke up. Then a great wave of alarm spread over the city. Not one of the costumes would come off then. The buttons buttoned as fast as they were unbuttoned; the pins quilted themselves in as fast as they were pulled out; and the strings flew round like lightning and twisted themselves into bowknots as fast as they were untied.

And that was not the worst of it; every one of the

children seemed to have become, in reality, the character which he or she had assumed.

The Mayor's daughter declared she was going to tend her geese out in the pasture, and the shepherdesses sprang out of their little beds of down, throwing aside their silken quilts, and cried that they must go out and watch their sheep. The princesses jumped up from their straw pallets, and wanted to go to court; and all the rest of them likewise. Poor little Red Riding-hood sobbed and sobbed because she couldn't go and carry her basket to her grandmother, and as she didn't have any grandmother she couldn't go, of course, and her parents were very much troubled. It was all so mysterious and dreadful. The news spread very rapidly over the city, and soon a great crowd gathered around the new Costumer's shop, for everyone thought he must be responsible for all this mischief.

The shop door was locked; but they soon battered it down with stones. When they rushed in the Costumer was not there; he had disappeared with all his wares. Then they did not know what to do. But it was evident that they must do something before long for the state of affairs was growing worse and worse.

The Mayor's little daughter braced her back up against the tapestried wall, and planted her two feet in their thick shoes firmly. "I will go and tend my geese!" she kept crying. "I won't eat my breakfast! I won't go out in the park! I won't go to school. I'm going to tend my geese—I will, I will, I will!"

And the princesses trailed their rich trains over the

rough, unpainted floors in their parents' poor little huts, and held their crowned heads very high and demanded to be taken to court. The princesses were mostly geese-girls when they were their proper selves, and their geese were suffering, and their poor parents did not know what they were going to do, and they wrung their hands and wept as they gazed on their gorgeously appareled children.

Finally the Mayor called a meeting of the Aldermen, and they all assembled in the City Hall. Nearly every one of them had a son or a daughter who was a chimney-sweep, or a little watch-girl, or a shepherdess. They appointed a chairman and they took a great many votes, and contrary votes; but they did not agree on anything, until someone proposed that they consult the Wise Woman. Then they all held up their hands, and voted to, unanimously.

So the whole board of Aldermen set out, walking by twos, with the Mayor at their head, to consult the Wise Woman. The Aldermen were all very fleshy, and carried gold-headed canes which they swung very high at every step. They held their heads well back, and their chins stiff, and whenever they met common people they sniffed gently. They were very imposing.

The Wise Woman lived in a little hut on the outskirts of the city. She kept a Black Cat; except for her, she was all alone. She was very old, and had brought up a great many children, and she was considered remarkably wise.

But when the Aldermen reached her hut and found

her seated by the fire, holding her Black Cat, a new difficulty presented itself. She had always been quite deaf and people had been obliged to scream as loud as they could in order to make her hear; but lately she had grown much deafer, and when the Aldermen attempted to lay the case before her she could not hear a word. In fact, she was so very deaf that she could not distinguish a tone below G-sharp. The Aldermen screamed till they were quite red in the faces, but all to no purpose; none of them could get up to G-sharp of course.

So the Aldermen all went back, swinging their gold-headed canes, and they had another meeting in the City Hall. Then they decided to send the highest Soprano Singer in the church choir to the Wise Woman; she could sing up to G-sharp just as easy as not. So the high Soprano Singer set out for the Wise Woman's in the Mayor's coach, and the Aldermen marched behind, swinging their gold-headed canes.

The high Soprano Singer put her head down close to the Wise Woman's ear, and sang all about the Christmas Masquerade, and the dreadful dilemma everybody was in, in G-sharp—she even went higher, sometimes— and the Wise Woman heard every word. She nodded three times, and every time she nodded she looked a little wiser.

"Go home, and give 'em a spoonful of castor-oil, all 'round," she piped up; then she took a pinch of snuff, and wouldn't say any more.

So the Aldermen went home, and each one took a district and marched through it, with a servant carrying an immense bowl and spoon, and every child had to take a dose of castor-oil.

But it didn't do a bit of good. The children cried and struggled when they were forced to take the castor-oil; but, two minutes afterward, the chimney-sweeps were crying for their brooms, and the princesses screaming because they couldn't go to court, and the Mayor's daughter, who had been given a double dose, cried louder and more sturdily: "I want to go and tend my geese! I will go and tend my geese!"

So the Aldermen took the high Soprano Singer, and they consulted the Wise Woman again. She was taking a nap this time, and the Singer had to sing up to B-flat before she could wake her. Then she was very cross, and the Black Cat put up his back and spit at the Aldermen.

"Give 'em a spanking all 'round," she snapped out, "and if that don't work put 'em to bed without their supper."

Then the Aldermen marched back to try that; and all the children in the city were spanked, and when that didn't do any good they were put to bed without any supper. But the next morning when they woke up they were worse than ever.

The Mayor and Aldermen were very indignant, and considered that they had been imposed upon and insulted. So they set out for the Wise Woman's again, with the high Soprano Singer.

She sang in G-sharp how the Aldermen and the Mayor considered her an impostor, and did not think she was wise at all, and they wished her to take her Black

Cat and move beyond the limits of the city. She sang it beautifully; it sounded like the very finest Italian opera music.

"Deary me," piped the Wise Woman, when she had finished, "how very grand these gentlemen are." Her Black Cat put up his back and spit.

"Five times one Black Cat are five Black Cats," said the Wise Woman. And directly there were five Black Cats spitting and miauling.

"Five times five Black Cats are twenty-five Black Cats." And then there were twenty-five of the angry little beasts.

"Five times twenty-five Black Cats are one hundred and twenty-five Black Cats," added the Wise Woman with a chuckle.

Then the Mayor and the Aldermen and the high Soprano Singer fled precipitately out the door and back to the city. One hundred and twenty-five Black Cats had seemed to fill the Wise Woman's hut full, and when they all spit and miauled together it was dreadful. The visitors could not wait for her to multiply Black Cats any longer.

As winter wore on and spring came, the condition of things grew more intolerable. Physicians had been consulted, who advised that the children should be allowed to follow their own bents, for fear of injury to their constitutions. So the rich Aldermen's daughters were actually out in the fields herding sheep, and their sons were sweeping chimneys or carrying newspapers; while the poor charwomen's and coal-heavers' children spent their time like princesses and fairies. Such a topsy-turvy state of society was shocking. Why, the Mayor's little daughter was tending geese out in the meadow like any common goose-girl. Her pretty elder sister, Violetta, felt very sad about it and used often to cast about in her mind for some way of relief.

When cherries were ripe in spring, Violetta thought she would ask the Cherry-man about it. She thought the Cherry-man quite wise. He was a very pretty young fellow, and he brought cherries to sell in graceful little straw baskets lined with moss. So she stood in the kitchen door one morning and told him all about the great trouble that had come upon the city. He listened in great astonishment; he had never heard of it before. He lived several miles out in the country.

"How did the Costumer look?" he asked respectfully; he thought Violetta the most beautiful lady on earth.

Then Violetta described the Costumer, and told him of the unavailing attempts that had been made to find him. There were a great many detectives out, constantly at work.

"I know where he is!" said the Cherry-man. "He's up in one of my cherry trees. He's been living there ever since cherries were ripe, and he won't come down."

Then Violetta ran and told her father in great excitement, and he at once called a meeting of the Aldermen, and in a few hours half the city was on the road to the Cherry-man's.

He had a beautiful orchard of cherry trees, all laden

with fruit. And, sure enough, in one of the largest, way up amongst the topmost branches, sat the Costumer in his red velvet knee breeches and his diamond knee buckles. He looked down between the green boughs. "Good morning, friends!" he shouted.

The Aldermen shook their gold-headed canes at him, and the people danced round the tree in a rage. Then they began to climb. But they soon found that to be impossible. As fast as they touched a hand or foot to the tree, back it flew with a jerk exactly as if the tree pushed it. They tried a ladder, but the ladder fell back the moment it touched the tree, and lay sprawling upon the ground. Finally, they brought axes and thought they could chop the tree down, Costumer and all; but the wood resisted the axes as if it were iron, and only dented them, receiving no impression itself.

Meanwhile, the Costumer sat up in the tree, eating cherries and throwing the stones down. Finally he stood up on a stout branch, and, looking down, addressed the people.

"It's of no use, your trying to accomplish anything in this way," said he; "you'd better parley. I'm willing to come to terms with you, and make everything right on two conditions."

The people grew quiet then, and the Mayor stepped forward as spokesman, "Name your two conditions," said he rather testily. "You own, tacitly, that you are the cause of all this trouble."

"Well," said the Costumer, reaching out for a handful of cherries, "this Christmas Masquerade of yours was a beautiful idea; but you wouldn't do it every year, and your successors might not do it at all. I want those poor children to have a Christmas every year. My first condition is that every poor child in the city hangs his stocking for gifts in the City Hall on every Christmas Eve, and gets it filled, too. I want the resolution filed and put away in the city archives."

"We agree to the first condition!" cried the people with one voice, without waiting for the Mayor and Aldermen.

"The second condition," said the Costumer, "is that this good young Cherry-man here has the Mayor's daughter, Violetta, for his wife. He has been kind to me, letting me live in his cherry tree and eat his cherries, and I want to reward him."

"We consent!" cried all the people; but the Mayor, though he was so generous, was a proud man. "I will not consent to the second condition," he cried angrily.

"Very well," replied the Costumer, picking some more cherries, "Then your youngest daughter tends geese the rest of her life, that's all."

The Mayor was in great distress; but the thought of his youngest daughter being a goose-girl all her life was too much for him. He gave in at last.

"Now go home and take the costumes off your children," said the Costumer, "and leave me in peace to eat cherries."

Then the people hastened back to the city and found, to their great delight, that the costumes would come off. The pins stayed out, the buttons stayed unbuttoned, and the strings stayed untied. The children were dressed in their own proper clothes and were their own proper selves once more. The shepherdesses and the chimney-sweeps came home, and were washed and dressed in silks and velvets, and went to embroidering and playing lawn tennis. And the princesses and the fairies put on their own suitable dresses, and went about their useful employments. There was great rejoicing in every home. Violetta thought she had never been so happy, now that her dear little sister was no longer a goose-girl, but her own dainty little lady-self.

The resolution to provide every poor child in the

city with a stocking full of gifts on Christmas was solemnly filed, and deposited in the city archives, and was never broken.

Violetta was married to the Cherry-man, and all the children came to the wedding, and strewed flowers in her path till her feet were quite hidden in them. The Costumer had mysteriously disappeared from the cherry tree the night before, but he left at the foot some beautiful wedding presents for the bride—a silver service with a pattern of cherries engraved on it, and a set of china with cherries on it, in hand painting, and a white satin robe, embroidered with cherries down the front.

The Runaway Christmas Bus

Florence Page Jaques

He was such a funny, sweet-tempered, jolly old motor bus, Number 999 was. He was so very wide and so very steady, and his bright paint always looked so fresh and shiny that you loved the first glimpse you had of him.

He never pretended not to see people when they wanted him to stop at a corner. He wouldn't have dreamed of such a thing! He always stopped and waited till they got on with both feet. He never skidded sideways on slippery days, as some of the younger busses liked to do. He went rumbling straight along and never broke down.

Everybody liked Number 999; and Number 999 liked everybody, from the tiny little babies who looked so surprised to be there, to the old, old men who always carried their canes and their white whiskers with them.

But one morning Number 999 started out, and he didn't feel like himself at all!

It was a lovely, cold, snowy morning, with great white snowflakes like butterflies in the air, and a soft gray sky. And everybody seemed so happy, with bundles and holly and twinkles in their arms and buttonholes and faces.

There were round green wreaths and bright red ribbons on doors and bells jingling down the streets. The shop windows were packed with scarlet and green and gold, and there was a smell of pine trees in the air which made Number 999 feel like a little play bus again, somehow. "Why do I feel like that?" he wondered. "It smells like—like Christmas trees!" And just then a gay little boy's voice said, "It will be a snowy Christmas tomorrow, Daddy!"

"Why," said Number 999 to himself, "it's the day before Christmas!"

Now, Number 999 always worked harder at Christmas time than any other time. Everybody in the world was scurrying around then, shopping at the last minute, and losing their packages, and having to go back again, and going to see their grandmothers and cousins and children and aunts and mothers and fathers, (according to their age, you know), and carrying big parcels with exciting ends sticking out, a doll's foot or a velocipede handle or a long scarlet candle. Number 999 had very heavy loads.

But he adored Christmas time just the same. And best of all he liked the day before Christmas. It seemed the gayest and the most adventurous, and the fullest of delightful secrets of all the days!

But this particular day before Christmas, as I said, Number 999 felt very odd. He had never felt just this way before in his whole life! Somehow he didn't want to carry everybody back and forth to their merry Christmases. He wanted to have a day before Christmas himself!

All at once, there in the middle of the street, he gave a jump, up in the air, with all four wheels. "I'm *going* to have a Christmas myself," he said. "I'm going to run away!"

And without even thinking another minute about it, he started off! He ran down the snowy street just as fast as he could, and though there was a nice old lady waiting for him on the very first corner, he didn't even wink! He just tossed his head, and laughed deep down in his radiator, and ran on faster than ever.

He had never done that before! He had always stopped for everybody.

He was as bad as he could be, that day before Christmas. He ran all over town, and nobody could stop him! He didn't pay the least attention to the traffic cops—he ran around just as he liked!

He got the streetcars and trucks all mixed up by running down the wrong side of the street. He tooted his horn unexpectedly at people and made them jump out of their rubbers. He stood up on his back wheels and *lunged* at a very fat young man, with a flower in his coat and a beautiful new hat. And the very fat young man ran and lost his flower *and* his hat. And Number 999 laughed till he choked. Yes, he did—good old Number 999, who had always been so kind!

He picked up a holly wreath with a bright red ribbon bow, and stuck it over one ear. Then he looked at himself in a big store window and pranced in the street, because he was so proud. Then he started off to run faster than ever! Nobody could do one thing with him!

The Policeman tried to stop him; so did the Chief of Police; so did the Mayor. But Number 999 just laughed and laughed and blew his horn and ran around the corner.

At last the Mayor ordered *all* the police, especially the two on horseback, and *all* the fire departments, especially the hook and ladder, and the band, and the patrol wagon, to assemble in the square, by the big outdoor Christmas tree.

"We'll have to catch Number 999, and put him in jail," the Mayor said sternly.

Number 999 decided, suddenly, that he had played long enough in the city. So he ran away, out into the country.

Oh, what a good time he had out there! For he was a city bus—he had never been in the country before— and he *liked* running along a country road in the snow, with no one else in sight, and his horn sounding so

loudly in the still blue air. He felt more and more excited!

Then he found a steep hill, and he lay down on his back with his wheels in the air, and slid down it! Then he rolled over and over in the fluffy snowdrifts, first taking off his holly wreath and hanging it up on a tree.

Then he found a little river all covered with ice, and he slid up and down it for a long time. Then he went back to find his holly wreath, and he put it on, and started down the winding road again. He skipped.

After a while he saw the high and mighty walls of

a castle, up on a hilltop. He stopped a green wagon which was ambling slowly by.

"What is that, on that hill, over there?" he asked.

"What?" said the wagon.

"That castle on the hill—what is it?" Number 999 asked the green wagon a second time.

"It's a castle," said the wagon.

"Of course it is, old slab sides," said Number 999, laughing. "But who lives there?"

"The Lord of the Castle lives there," said the wagon slowly, after a long silence. "All alone he lives, since his daughter married the piper, and he sent them away."

"I believe I'll just run up and see him," said the motor bus.

"I'll watch for you to come down," said the green wagon. It gave a low, deep chuckle, and started slowly on again.

Number 999 ran up the steep hill to the castle gates. He had to go so fast to get up the hill at all that, when he ran inside the castle gates, he couldn't stop. He ran on, through the castle door, and—*bang!*—into the great crystal mirror in the Hall of State, and he shattered it to bits. Nothing was left but the gold frame, and it was hanging around Number 999's neck!

The Lord of the Castle came rushing out from lunch with a blueberry muffin in his hand. Oh, how angry he was! He threw the muffin violently at Number 999, and he called to all his soldiers, "Arrest that motor bus!"

Number 999 ran round and round the Hall of State,

and the soldiers ran after him, tripping on the crimson cord that hung from the mirror frame.

But at last Number 999 crashed into a marble column accidentally—a muffin crumb had gone in his eye —and he sat down with a thump. Then all the soldiers seized him (he was so stunned by the crash that he couldn't even wiggle) and they *threw* him out of the castle gates and he rolled down the steep castle hill.

Number 999 heard a faint giggle as the green wagon passed slowly behind a hill in the distance.

The soldiers had barred the gates, and the Lord of the Castle stood on the gray wall in his purple cloak and shook his fist at Number 999, who sat in the ditch and rubbed his forehead and straightened his holly wreath.

"If you ever come back again," said the Lord of the Castle, "I'll have you chopped up in little pieces. In pieces!"

The motor bus climbed stiffly out of the ditch and started off again. All at once he began to laugh. "I wish I could have seen myself falling down the hill!" he said.

By this time it was almost dark. It was very quiet along the country road, and the snow lay white on the hills, and the great silver Christmas star shone in the sky. "It's Christmas Eve," said the motor bus to himself softly, and suddenly all the mischief left his heart, and something else came into it. He looked up at the Christmas star again, shining in the dark, clear sky.

"It's Christmas Eve," said the motor bus, and he began to sing a Christmas carol. But he stopped soon, for he loved music.

Then he heard a real Christmas carol coming through the air. And he followed the singing, and at last, just as it was really dark, he came to a little brown house, almost covered with snow. Round and round he prowled, till he found a window with the shade only half pulled down. Then he kneeled down on his front wheels and peeped through the window.

There was a rosy fire in the fireplace of the little house, and sitting before it was the loveliest lady he had ever seen, with three little girls on one side of her, and three little boys on the other. And they were all singing Christmas carols. The motor bus liked listening to their songs.

At last the lovely lady said, "Now, darlings, you must run away to bed. And remember, though tomorrow is Christmas Day, there won't be any Christmas presents. Are you *sure* you won't mind?"

"Of course, we won't mind, Mother," said the oldest little boy sturdily. "We think you're wonderful. You've made enough money sewing to get our bread and milk, even though you do have to work all the time." Number 999 looked, and indeed the lovely lady was sewing even then.

"We all think the Christmas carols are a lovely Christmas present," said the middle little boy.

"Are you sure the Lord of the Castle won't send Christmas presents?" said the littlest little boy wistfully.

"Of course, he won't," said the oldest little girl. "He doesn't know that Daddy had to go way off to the other side of the world to get money enough for us."

"I know," said the littlest girl, "how you can give us a Christmas present tomorrow, Mother. You can tell us about the wonderful Christmases you had when you were the Lord of the Castle's little girl!"

"That's what I'll do," said the lovely lady, laughing. But when all the children were asleep in bed, she sat by the fire and cried because there were no Christmas presents for them.

Oh, the motor bus simply couldn't bear to see the lady crying! It hurt him somewhere inside. And when he thought of all the things the Lord of the Castle had, it made him so mad that his engine whirred faster and faster. Then, all at once, he had a wonderful idea!

It was such a good idea that Number 999 could hardly keep from sounding his horn. He could hardly keep his wheels still. But he waited patiently till the lady went to sleep, there by the fire.

Then—he slipped around to the front of the house, and he pulled a strong rope out of the tool box, and he tied one end of it around the little brown house, and the other around his waist, and he began to pull the little brown house down the snowy road!

Down the road they went and through the snow, till they came to the Castle hill. The bus had a dreadful time pulling the little brown house up that steep hill! But at last he did.

Then he opened the castle gates gently, and he left the little brown house in the courtyard. He went on into the castle—only carefully this time, so that he wouldn't break anything—and into the banquet hall where the

Lord of the Castle and all the soldiers were having a feast.

"There's that ridiculous motor bus," shouted the Lord of the Castle angrily. "Didn't I tell him I'd have him chopped up in little pieces if he ever came back?"

"Well, you can have me chopped up in little pieces," said the motor bus bravely, though his windows shook at the thought. "But first I have something to show you."

So he led the Lord of the Castle out into the court-yard and showed him the little brown house, and the three little girls and the three little boys asleep in their beds, and their mother asleep by the fire, and not a single Christmas present in the house.

The Lord of the Castle wanted to cry, but he couldn't, because he was Lord of the Castle. So he walked up and down the courtyard very fast, stamping his feet. Then he slapped the motor bus on the side.

"You're a good old bus, after all," he said. "Thank you for bringing them up."

Then he called to his soldiers, and everyone hurried.

In the morning, when the lady and the children woke up, it seemed unusually warm in the little brown house, which was most frightfully cold on winter mornings. And when they looked out a window, they seemed to see walls and banners instead of snow and fields! It seemed queer. So as soon as they were dressed they opened their door.

The little brown house had been moved again in

the night. It was inside the Hall of State, which was big enough to hold ten little brown houses!

When the lady and the children walked out of the front door, there was a great fireplace with a huge fire roaring in it, and a stocking apiece hanging, crammed full! In one corner was an enormous Christmas tree, green and silver and sparkling, with playthings, and candy and nuts, and every single thing a Christmas tree should have, hanging on it. And in the other corner was the motor bus, still with his holly wreath on, and Christmas tree ornaments all over him to make him look gay, and the biggest smile on his face that you ever did see! And there was a lovely turkey-cranberry-ice-cream-plum pudding smell coming around the corner!

And best of all, there was the Lord of the Castle, with open arms, in front of the fireplace!

The lovely lady laughed and cried and laughed again, and the Lord of the Castle hugged her and each little girl and each little boy. And then they had the stockings and then breakfast, and then the tree, and then dinner, and everybody said it was the nicest Christmas ever!

Forever after the lady and her three little boys and three little girls lived with the Lord of the Castle, and when her husband, the piper, came back from the other side of the world, he lived there, too.

And Number 999? Why, of course, he stayed! They all loved him as hard as they could. He had a green wreath to wear every day, and a gold one for Sundays.

And he asked them if they would call him Jimmy once in a while, and they did! And he never had to carry anyone around unless he wanted to, except the Lord of the Castle when he went into town to call on the Mayor. And he liked that.

The motor bus has been very happy ever since. But once in a while when he gets tired of playing around the castle, he goes down into the city and pretends to be a regular hard-working bus. Maybe you've ridden on him sometimes! He likes specially to take children and he likes the most of all to take them at Christmas time!

ALL ABOUT SANTA CLAUS

On Christmas Eve

Stella Mead

When the night goes gray and the stars are gold,
    When bells for Christmas ring,
When the children close by the Yuletide log
    Their Christmas carols sing;
In his sleigh he jumps, to the deer he calls,
    Away to earth he flies,
Through the crystal stars of the Milky Way
    And down the silver skies.

      He is Santa Claus in a crimson gown,
        With a beard so white and long,
      We will sound his praise to the chimney-tops
        In a rousing Christmas song.

He has glittering toys in his tinkling sleigh
    For little ones on earth,
There are smiles in his eyes as he drives along;
    His cheeks are round with mirth.
He has presents packed for the grown-up folk
    With sprigs of mistletoe.
And the reindeer rush with their jingling bells—
    Ring-ting, ring-tang, ring-O!

      He is Santa Claus in a crimson gown,
        With a beard so white and long,
      We will sound his praise to the chimney-tops
        In a rousing Christmas song.

He will leave his deer on the snowy roof,
    And softly he will creep
To the small white beds where the children lie
    Half-smiling in their sleep.
For the children know that on Christmas Eve
    Their friend is on his way,
And they dream all night of a red-gowned man
    In a tinkling-jingling sleigh.

      He is Santa Claus in a crimson gown,
        With a beard so white and long,
      We will sound his praise to the chimney-tops
        In a rousing Christmas song.

Santa Claus

A Wonder Story for Little Children

Maud Lindsay

"Wonder is the basis of worship."—*Carlyle*.

Every year, on the night before Christmas, Santa Claus comes.

He rides in a sleigh drawn by tiny reindeer with bells on their harnesses.

Tinkle, tinkle, ring the bells, and trit-trot, go the little deer to carry Santa Claus over the world.

Santa Claus dresses in fur from his head to his heels. His leggings are fur, his coat is fur, and he wears a fur cap pulled down over his ears, for the winds of winter are icy cold.

O-o-o-o, sing the winds, tink, tinkle, ring the bells, and trit-trot, go the little deer when Santa Claus rides over the world.

Santa Claus's beard is as white as the snow, and his cheeks are as red as apples, and his eyes are as bright as the twinkling stars that look from the sky to see him ride.

Twinkle, twinkle, shine the stars, O-o-o-o, sing the winds, tink, tinkle, ring the bells, and trit-trot, go the little deer when Santa Claus rides over the world.

Santa is old, old as the hills, but he is strong as a giant, and on his back he carries a pack, and the pack is full of toys. He has dolls and drums, and balls and tops, wagons and sleds, tea sets with blue roses painted on them, and horns with red and white stripes; and all of them are for little children. As soon as the children are asleep on Christmas Eve, Santa Claus comes to fill their stockings with good things and give them beautiful gifts. He knows just what the children want, every one of them, and he laughs for joy as he rides away.

Ha! Ha! laughs Santa Claus, twinkle, twinkle, shine the stars, O-o-o-o, sing the winds, tink, tinkle, ring the bells, and trit-trot, go the little deer when Santa Claus rides over the world.

The children never see him come. No, indeed! If he hears so much as a laugh or a whisper in the house he stays outside till all is quiet. Why, once upon a time there was a little boy who did not want to go to bed on the night before Christmas. "I shall sit up and see Santa Claus," he said. He hung his stocking on the mantel, and

sat in his mother's big rocking chair and waited, and watched, and waited; but all that he saw was a little gray mouse, though he stayed awake till everybody but his mother was in bed, and he could not keep his eyes open another minute. The last thing he saw as he went to sleep was the stocking hanging just where he had put it, and there was nothing in it; but—do you believe it?— when he waked up next morning it was full of goodies from tip to toe; and right in front of the hearth was a wagon with red wheels! "Oh, oh! Santa Claus has been here," said the little boy; and he clapped his hands, for he was happy as could be.

All the world is happy when Santa Claus comes. Trit-trot, go the little deer, tink, tinkle, ring the bells, O-o-o-o, sing the winds, twinkle, twinkle, shine the stars, and ha! ha! laughs Santa Claus, as he rides over the world to fill the children's stockings, and to bring beautiful gifts.

Behind the White Brick

Frances Hodgson Burnett

Jem knew what to expect when Aunt Hetty began a day by calling her "Jemima." It was one of the poor child's grievances that she had been given such an ugly name. In all the books she had read, and she had read a great many, Jem never had met a heroine who was called Jemima. But it had been her mother's favorite sister's name, and so it had fallen to her lot. Her mother always called her "Jem," or "Mimi," which was much prettier, and even Aunt Hetty only reserved Jemima for unpleasant state occasions.

It was a dreadful day to Jem. Her mother was not at home, and would not be until night. She had been called away unexpectedly, and had been obliged to leave Jem and the baby to Aunt Hetty's mercies.

So Jem found herself busy enough. Scarcely had she finished doing one thing, when Aunt Hetty told her to begin another. She wiped dishes and picked fruit and attended to the baby; and when baby had gone to sleep, and everything else seemed disposed of, for a time, at least, she was so tired that she was glad to sit down.

And then she thought of the book she had been reading the night before—a certain delightful storybook, about a little girl whose name was Flora, and who was so happy and rich and pretty and good that Jem had likened her to the little princesses one reads about.

"I shall have time to finish my chapter before dinnertime comes," said Jem, and she sat down snugly in one corner of the wide, old-fashioned fireplace.

But she had not read more than two pages before something dreadful happened. Aunt Hetty came into the room in a great hurry—in such a hurry, indeed, that she caught her foot in the matting and fell, striking her elbow sharply against a chair, which so upset her temper that the moment she found herself on her feet she flew at Jem.

"What!" she said, snatching the book from her. "Reading again, when I am running all over the house for you?" And she flung the pretty little blue-covered volume into the fire.

Jem sprang to rescue it with a cry, but it was impossible to reach it; it had fallen into a great hollow of red coal, and the blaze caught it at once.

"You are a wicked woman!" cried Jem, in a dreadful passion, to Aunt Hetty. "You are a very wicked woman."

Then matters reached a climax. Aunt Hetty boxed her ears, pushed her back on her little footstool, and walked out of the room.

Jem hid her face on her arms and cried as if her heart would break. She cried until her eyes were heavy, but just as she was thinking of going to sleep, something fell down the chimney and made her look up. It was a piece of mortar, and she bent forward and looked up to see where it had come from. The chimney was so very wide that this was easy enough. She could see where the mortar had fallen from the side and left a white patch.

"How white it looks against the black," said Jem, "it is like a white brick among the black ones. What a queer place a chimney is!"

And then a funny thought came into her fanciful little head. How many things were burned in the big fireplace and vanished in smoke or tinder up the chimney! Where did everything go? There was Flora, for instance—Flora who was represented on the frontispiece —with lovely, soft, flowing hair, and a little fringe on her pretty round forehead, crowned with a circlet of daisies, and a laugh in her wide-awake round eyes. Where was she by this time? Certainly there was nothing left of her in the fire. Jem almost began to cry again at the thought.

"It was too bad," she said. "She was so pretty and funny, and I did like her so."

I dare say it scarcely will be credited by unbelieving

people when I tell them what happened next . . . Jem felt herself gradually lifted off her little footstool.

"Oh!" she said, timidly, "how—how very light I feel! Oh, dear, I'm going up the chimney . . . I've heard Aunt Hetty talk about the draught drawing things up the chimney, but I never knew it was as strong as this."

She went up, up, up, quietly and steadily, and without any uncomfortable feeling at all; and then all at once she stopped, feeling that her feet rested against something solid. She opened her eyes and looked about her, and there she was, standing right opposite the white brick, her feet on a tiny ledge.

"Well," she said, "this is funny."

But the next thing that happened was funnier still. She found that, without thinking what she was doing, she was knocking on the white brick with her knuckles, as if it was a door and she expected somebody to open it. The next minute she heard footsteps, and then a sound, as if someone was drawing back a little bolt.

"It is a door," said Jem, "and somebody is going to open it."

The white brick moved a little, and some more mortar and soot fell; then the brick moved a little more, and then it slid aside and left an open space.

"It's a room!" cried Jem. "There's a room behind it!"

And so there was, and before the open space stood a pretty little girl, with long lovely hair and a fringe on her forehead. Jem clasped her hands in amazement. It was Flora herself, as she looked in the picture.

"Come in," she said. "I thought it was you."

"But how can I come in through such a little place?" asked Jem.

"Oh, that is easy enough," said Flora. "Here, give me your hand."

Jem did as she told her, and found that it was easy enough. In an instant she had passed through the opening, the white brick had gone back to its place, and she was standing by Flora's side in a large room—the nicest room she had ever seen. It was big and lofty and light, and there were all kinds of delightful things in it—books and flowers and playthings and pictures, and in one corner a great cage full of lovebirds.

"Have I ever seen it before?" asked Jem, glancing slowly round.

"Why," said Flora, laughing, "it's my room, the one you read about last night."

"So it is," said Jem. "But how did you come here?"

"I can't tell you that; I myself don't know. But I am here, and so"—rather mysteriously—"are a great many other things."

"Are they?" said Jem, very much interested. "What things? Burned things? I was just wondering——"

"Not only burned things," said Flora, nodding. "Just come with me and I'll show you something."

She led the way out of the room and down a little passage with several doors in each side of it, and she opened one door and showed Jem what was on the other side of it. That was a room, too, and this time it was funny as well as pretty. Both floor and walls were padded

with rose color, and the floor was strewn with toys. There were big soft balls, rattles, horses, woolly dogs, and a doll or so; there was one low cushioned chair and a low table.

"You can come in," said a shrill little voice behind the door, "only mind you don't tread on things."

"What a funny little voice!" said Jem, but she had no sooner said it than she jumped back.

The owner of the voice, who had just come forward, was no other than Baby.

"Why," exclaimed Jem, beginning to feel frightened, "I left you fast asleep in your crib."

"Did you?" said Baby, somewhat scornfully. "That's just the way with you grown-up people. You think you know everything, and yet you haven't discretion enough to know when a pin is sticking into one.

You'd know soon enough if you had one sticking into your own back."

"But I'm not grown up," stammered Jem; "and when you are at home you can neither walk nor talk. You're not six months old."

"Well, Miss," retorted Baby, whose wrongs seemed to have soured her disposition somewhat, "you have no need to throw that in my teeth; you were not six months old, either, when you were my age."

Jem could not help laughing.

"You haven't got any teeth," she said.

"Haven't I?" said Baby, and she displayed two beautiful rows with some haughtiness of manner. "When I am up here," she said, "I am supplied with the modern conveniences, and that's why I never complain. Do I ever cry when I am asleep? It's not falling asleep I object to, it's falling awake."

"Wait a minute," said Jem. "Are you asleep now?"

"I'm what you call asleep. I can only come here when I'm what you call asleep. Asleep, indeed! It's no wonder we always cry when we have to fall awake."

"But we don't mean to be unkind to you," protested Jem, meekly.

She could not help thinking Baby was very severe.

"Don't mean!" said Baby. "Well, why don't you think more, then? How would you like to have all the nice things snatched away from you, and all the old rubbish packed off on you, as if you hadn't any sense? How would you like to have to sit and stare at things you wanted, and not to be able to reach them, or, if you did reach them, have them fall out of your hand, and roll away in the most unfeeling manner? And then be scolded and called 'cross'! It's no wonder we are bald. You'd be bald yourself. It's trouble and worry that keep us bald until we can begin to take care of ourselves; I had more hair than this at first, but it fell off, as well it might. No philosopher ever thought of that, I suppose!"

"Well," said Jem, in despair, "I hope you enjoy yourself when you are here."

"Yes, I do," answered Baby. "That's one comfort. There is nothing to knock my head against, and things have patent stoppers on them, so that they can't roll away, and everything is soft and easy to pick up."

There was a slight pause after this, and Baby seemed to cool down.

"I suppose you would like me to show you round?" she said.

"Not if you have any objection," replied Jem, who was rather subdued.

"I would as soon do it as not," said Baby. "You are not as bad as some people, though you do get my clothes twisted when you hold me."

Upon the whole, she seemed rather proud of her position. It was evident she quite regarded herself as hostess. She held her small bald head very high indeed, as she trotted on before them. She stopped at the first door she came to, and knocked three times. She was obliged to stand upon tiptoe to reach the knocker.

"He's sure to be at home at this time of year," she remarked. "This is the busy season."

"Who's 'he'?" inquired Jem.

But Flora only laughed at Miss Baby's consequential air.

"S. C., to be sure," was the answer, as the young lady pointed to the doorplate, upon which Jem noticed, for the first time, "S. C." in very large letters.

The door opened, apparently without assistance, and they entered the apartment.

"Good gracious!" exclaimed Jem, the next minute. "Good*ness* gracious!"

She might well be astonished. It was such a long room that she could not see to the end of it, and it was piled up from floor to ceiling with toys of every description, and there was such bustle and buzzing in it that it was quite confusing. The bustle and buzzing arose from a very curious cause, too,—it was the bustle and buzz of hundreds of tiny men and women who were working at little tables no higher than mushrooms,—the pretty tiny women cutting out and sewing, the pretty tiny men sawing and hammering and all talking at once. The principal person in the place escaped Jem's notice at first; but it was not long before she saw him,—a little old gentleman, with a rosy face and sparkling eyes, sitting at a desk, and writing in a book almost as big as himself. He was so busy that he was quite excited, and had been obliged to throw his white fur coat and cap aside, and he was at work in his red waistcoat.

"Look here, if you please," piped Baby. "I have brought someone to see you."

When he turned round, Jem recognized him.

"Eh! Eh!" he said. "What! What! Who's this, Tootsicums?"

Baby's manner became very acid indeed.

"I shouldn't have thought you would have said that, Mr. Claus," she remarked. "I can't help myself down below, but I generally have my rights respected up here."

"Come, come!" said S. C., chuckling comfortably and rubbing his hands. "Don't be too dignified,—it's a bad thing. And don't be too fond of flourishing your rights in people's faces,—that's the worst of all, Miss Midget. Folks who make such a fuss about their rights turn them into wrongs sometimes."

Then he turned suddenly to Jem.

"You are the little girl from down below," he said.

"Yes, sir," answered Jem. "I'm Jem, and this is my friend Flora,—out of the blue book."

"I'm happy to make her acquaintance," said S. C., "and I'm happy to make yours. You are a nice child, though a trifle peppery. I'm very glad to see you."

"I'm very glad indeed to see you, sir," said Jem. "I wasn't quite sure——"

But there she stopped, feeling that it would be scarcely polite to tell him that she had begun of late years to lose faith in him.

But S. C. only chuckled more comfortably than ever and rubbed his hands again.

"Ho, ho!" he said. "You know who I am, then?"

Jem hesitated a moment, wondering whether it would not be taking a liberty to mention his name without putting "Mr." before it; then she remembered what Baby had called him.

"Baby called you 'Mr. Claus,' sir," she replied; "and I have seen pictures of you."

"To be sure," said S. C. "S. Claus, Esquire, of Chimneyland. How do you like me?"

"Very much," answered Jem; "very much, indeed, sir."

"Glad of it! Glad of it! But what was it you were going to say you were not quite sure of?"

Jem blushed a little.

"I was not quite sure that—that you were true, sir. At least I have not been quite sure since I have been older."

S. C. rubbed the bald part of his head and gave a little sigh.

"I hope I have not hurt your feelings, sir," faltered Jem, who was a very kind-hearted little soul.

"Well, no," said S. C. "Not exactly. And it is not your fault either. It is natural, I suppose; at any rate, it is the way of the world. People lose their belief in a great many things as they grow older; but that does not make the things not true, thank goodness! and their faith often comes back after a while. But, bless me!" he added, briskly, "I'm moralizing, and who thanks a man for doing that? Suppose——"

"Black eyes or blue, sir?" said a tiny voice close to them.

Jem and Flora turned round, and saw it was one of the small workers who was asking the question.

"Whom for?" inquired S. C.

"Little girl in the red brick house at the corner," said the workwoman; "name of Birdie."

"Excuse me a moment," said S. C. to the children, and he turned to the big book and began to run his fingers down the pages in a business-like manner. "Ah! here she is!" he exclaimed at last. "Blue eyes, if you please, Thistle, and golden hair. And let it be a big one. She takes good care of them."

"Yes, sir," said Thistle; "I am personally acquainted with several dolls in her family. I go to parties in her dolls' house sometimes when she is fast asleep at night, and they all speak very highly of her. She is most attentive to them when they are ill. In fact, her pet doll is a cripple, with a stiff leg."

She ran back to her work and S. C. finished his sentence.

"Suppose I show you my establishment," he said. "Come with me."

It really would be quite impossible to describe the wonderful things he showed them. Jem's head was quite in a whirl before she had seen one-half of them, and even Baby condescended to become excited.

"There must be a great many children in the world, Mr. Claus," ventured Jem.

"Yes, yes, millions of 'em; bless 'em," said S. C., growing rosier with delight at the very thought. "We never run out of them, that's one comfort. There's a large and varied assortment always on hand. Fresh ones every year, too, so that when one grows too old there is a new one ready. I have a place like this in every twelfth chimney. Now it's boys, now it's girls, always one or t'other; and there's no end of playthings for them, too, I'm glad to say. For girls, the great thing seems to be dolls. Blitzen! what comfort they *do* take in dolls! but the boys are for horses and racket."

They were standing near a table where a worker was just putting the finishing touch to the dress of a large wax doll, and just at that moment, to Jem's surprise, she set it on the floor, upon its feet, quite coolly.

"Thank you," said the doll, politely.

Jem quite jumped.

"You can join the rest now and introduce yourself," said the worker.

The doll looked over her shoulder at her train.

"It hangs very nicely," she said. "I hope it's the latest fashion."

"Mine never talked like that," said Flora. "My best one could only say 'Mamma,' and it said it very badly, too."

"She was foolish for saying it at all," remarked the doll, haughtily. "We don't talk and walk before ordinary people; we keep our accomplishments for our own amusement, and for the amusement of our friends. If you should chance to get up in the middle of the night, some time, or should run into the room suddenly some day, after you have left it, you might hear—but what is the use of talking to human beings?"

"You know a great deal, considering you are only just finished," snapped Baby, who really was a Tartar.

"I was FINISHED," retorted the doll. "I did not begin life as a baby!" very scornfully.

"Pooh!" said Baby. "We improve as we get older."

"I hope so, indeed," answered the doll. "There is plenty of room for improvement." And she walked away in great state.

S. C. looked at Baby and then shook his head. "I shall not have to take very much care of you," he said, absent-mindedly. "You are able to take pretty good care of yourself."

"I hope I am," said Baby, tossing her head.

S. C. gave his head another shake.

"Don't take too good care of yourself," he said. "That's a bad thing, too."

He showed them the rest of his wonders, and then went with them to the door to bid them good-by.

"I am sure we are very much obliged to you, Mr. Claus," said Jem, gratefully. "I shall never again think you are not true, sir."

S. C. patted her shoulder quite affectionately.

"That's right," he said. "Believe in things just as

long as you can, my dear. Good-by until Christmas Eve. I shall see you then, if you don't see me."

He must have taken quite a fancy to Jem, for he stood looking at her, and seemed very reluctant to close the door, and even after he had closed it, and they had turned away, he opened it a little again to call to her.

"Believe in things as long as you can, my dear."

"How kind he is!" exclaimed Jem, full of pleasure.

And then, suddenly, a very strange feeling came over Jem. Without being able to account for it at all, she found herself sitting on her little stool again, with a beautiful scarlet and gold book on her knee, and her mother standing by laughing at her amazed face. As to Miss Baby, she was crying as hard as she could in her crib.

"Mother!" Jem cried out, "have you really come home so early as this, and—and," rubbing her eyes in great amazement, "how did I come down?"

"Don't I look as if I was real?" said her mother, laughing and kissing her. "And doesn't your present look real? I don't know how you came down, I'm sure. Where have you been?"

Jem shook her head very mysteriously. She saw that her mother fancied she had been asleep, but she herself knew better.

"I know you wouldn't believe it was true if I told you," she said; "I have been

BEHIND THE WHITE BRICK."

CHRISTMAS FUN AND NONSENSE

Lord Octopus Went to the Christmas Fair

Stella Mead

Lord Octopus went to the Christmas Fair;
An hour and a half he was traveling there.
    Then he had to climb
    For a weary time
    To the slimy block
    Of a sandstone rock,
    And creep, creep away
    To the big wide bay
    Where a stout old whale
    Held his Christmas Sale.

Lord Octopus went to the Christmas Fair;
An hour and a half he was traveling there.

His two little girls and two little boys
Were waiting at home for their Christmas toys;
  And dear old Granny,
  And fat Aunt Fanny,
  And Cousin Dolly,
  And Sister Molly
Would think Lord Octopus quite unpleasant
Unless he brought them a Christmas present.

Lord Octopus went to the Christmas Fair;
An hour and a half he was traveling there.
He purchased two hoops for the little boys.
He purchased two rings for the girls, as toys.
  He bought for Granny
  A sweet nightcap,
  To please Aunt Fanny
  A game of snap;
  For Cousin Dolly
  A winter wrap,
  For Sister Molly
  A sea-route map.
With hoops for the boys, for the girls round rings,
The wrap, and the rest of the Christmas things,
Tied up into parcels and packets strong,
Lord Octopus merrily went along.
On every arm he hung a present,
And said, "It's really rather pleasant
To have eight arms instead of two.
What can those human creatures do
With just two arms for all the toys
They have to buy their girls and boys?"

The Peterkins' Christmas Tree

Lucretia P. Hale

Early in autumn the Peterkins began to prepare for their Christmas tree. Everything was done in great privacy, as it was to be a surprise to the neighbors, as well as to the rest of the family. Mr. Peterkin had been up to Mr. Bromwick's woodlot, and, with his consent, selected the tree. Agamemnon went to look at it occasionally after dark, and Solomon John made frequent visits to it mornings, just after sunrise. Mr. Peterkin drove Elizabeth Eliza and her mother that way, and pointed furtively to it with his whip; but none of them ever spoke of it to each other. It was suspected that the little boys had been to see it Wednesday and Saturday afternoons.

But they came home with their pockets full of chestnuts, and said nothing about it.

At length Mr. Peterkin had it cut down and brought secretly into the Larkins' barn. A week or two before Christmas a measurement was made of it with Elizabeth Eliza's yard-measure. To Mr. Peterkin's great dismay it was discovered that it was too high to stand in the back parlor.

This fact was brought out at a secret council of Mr. and Mrs. Peterkin, Elizabeth Eliza, and Agamemnon.

Agamemnon suggested that it might be set up slanting; but Mrs. Peterkin was very sure it would make her dizzy, and the candles would drip.

But a brilliant idea came to Mr. Peterkin. He proposed that the ceiling of the parlor should be raised to make room for the top of the tree.

Elizabeth Eliza thought the space would need to be quite large. It must not be like a small box, or you could not see the tree.

"Yes," said Mr. Peterkin, "I should have the ceiling lifted all across the room; the effect would be finer."

Elizabeth Eliza objected to having the whole ceiling raised, because her room was over the back parlor, and she would have no floor while the alteration was going on, which would be very awkward. Besides, her room was not very high now, and, if the floor were raised, perhaps she could not walk in it upright.

Mr. Peterkin explained that he didn't propose altering the whole ceiling, but to lift up a ridge across the room at the back part where the tree was to stand. This

would make a hump, to be sure, in Elizabeth Eliza's room; but it would go across the whole room.

Elizabeth Eliza said she would not mind that. It would be like the cuddy thing that comes up on the deck of a ship, that you sit against, only here you would not have the sea-sickness. She thought she should like it, for a rarity. She might use it for a divan.

Mrs. Peterkin thought it would come in the worn place of the carpet, and might be a convenience in making the carpet over.

Agamemnon was afraid there would be trouble in keeping the matter secret, for it would be a long piece of work for a carpenter; but Mr. Peterkin proposed having the carpenter for a day or two, for a number of other jobs.

One of them was to make all the chairs in the house of the same height, for Mrs. Peterkin had nearly broken her spine by sitting down in a chair that she had supposed was her own rocking chair, and it had proved to be two inches lower. The little boys were now large enough to sit in any chair; so a medium was fixed upon to satisfy all the family, and the chairs were made uniformly of the same height.

On consulting the carpenter, however, he insisted that the tree could be cut off at the lower end to suit the height of the parlor, and demurred at so great a change as altering the ceiling. But Mr. Peterkin had set his mind upon the improvement, and Elizabeth Eliza had cut her carpet in preparation for it.

So the folding-doors into the back parlor were closed, and for nearly a fortnight before Christmas there was great litter of fallen plastering, and laths, and chips, and shavings; and Elizabeth Eliza's carpet was taken up, and the furniture had to be changed, and one night she had to sleep at the Bromwicks', for there was a long hole in her floor that might be dangerous.

All this delighted the little boys. They could not understand what was going on. Perhaps they suspected a Christmas tree, but they did not know why a Christmas tree should have so many chips, and were still more astonished at the hump that appeared in Elizabeth Eliza's room. It must be a Christmas present, or else the tree in a box.

Some aunts and uncles, too, arrived a day or two before Christmas, with some small cousins. These cousins occupied the attention of the little boys, and there was a great deal of whispering and mystery, behind doors, and under the stairs, and in the corners of the entry.

Solomon John was busy, privately making some candles for the tree. He had been collecting some bayberries, as he understood they made very nice candles, so that it would not be necessary to buy any.

The elders of the family never all went into the back parlor together, and all tried not to see what was going on. Mrs. Peterkin would go in with Solomon John, or Mr. Peterkin with Elizabeth Eliza, or Elizabeth Eliza and Agamemnon and Solomon John. The little boys and the small cousins were never allowed even to look inside the room.

Elizabeth Eliza meanwhile went into town a number of times. She wanted to consult Amanda as to how much ice cream they should need, and whether they could make it at home, as they had cream and ice. She was pretty busy in her own room; the furniture had to be changed, and the carpet altered. The "hump" was higher than she expected. There was danger of bumping her own head whenever she crossed it. She had to nail some padding on the ceiling for fear of accidents.

The afternoon before Christmas, Elizabeth Eliza, Solomon John, and their father collected in the back parlor for a council. The carpenters had done their work, and the tree stood at its full height at the back of the room, the top stretching up into the space arranged for it. All the chips and shavings were cleared away, and it stood on a neat box.

But what were they to put upon the tree?

Solomon John had brought in his supply of candles; but they proved to be very "stringy" and very few of them. It was strange how many bayberries it took to make a few candles! The little boys had helped him, and he had gathered as much as a bushel of bayberries. He had put them in water, and skimmed off the wax, according to the directions; but there was so little wax!

Solomon John had given the little boys some of the bits sawed off from the legs of the chairs. He had suggested that they should cover them with gilt paper, to answer for gilt apples, without telling them what they were for.

These apples, a little blunt at the end, and the candles, were all they had for the tree!

After all her trips into town Elizabeth Eliza had forgotten to bring anything for it.

"I thought of candies and sugar plums," she said; "but I concluded if we made caramels ourselves we should not need them. But, then, we have not made caramels. The fact is, that day my head was full of my carpet. I had bumped it pretty badly, too."

Mr. Peterkin wished he had taken, instead of a fir tree, an apple tree he had seen in October, full of red fruit.

"But the leaves would have fallen off by this time," said Elizabeth Eliza.

"And the apples, too," said Solomon John.

"It is odd I should have forgotten, that day I went in on purpose to get the things," said Elizabeth Eliza, musingly. "But I went from shop to shop, and didn't know exactly what to get. I saw a great many gilt things for Christmas trees; but I knew the little boys were making the gilt apples; there were plenty of candles in the shops, but I knew Solomon John was making the candles."

Mr. Peterkin thought it was quite natural.

Solomon John wondered if it were too late for them to go into town now.

Elizabeth Eliza could not go in the next morning, for there was to be a grand Christmas dinner, and Mr. Peterkin could not be spared, and Solomon John was sure he and Agamemnon would not know what to buy. Besides, they would want to try the candles tonight.

Mr. Peterkin asked if the presents everybody had been preparing would not answer. But Elizabeth Eliza knew they would be too heavy.

A gloom came over the room. There was only a

flickering gleam from one of Solomon John's candles that he had lighted by way of trial.

Solomon John again proposed going into town. He lighted a match to examine the newspaper about the trains. There were plenty of trains coming out at that hour, but none going in except a very late one. That would not leave time to do anything and come back.

"We could go in, Elizabeth Eliza and I," said Solomon John, "but we should not have time to buy anything."

Agamemnon was summoned in. Mrs. Peterkin was entertaining the uncles and aunts in the front parlor. Agamemnon wished there was time to study up something about electric lights. If they could only have a calcium light! Solomon John's candle sputtered and went out.

At this moment there was a loud knocking at the front door. The little boys, and the small cousins, and the uncles and aunts, and Mrs. Peterkin, hastened to see what was the matter.

The uncles and aunts thought somebody's house must be on fire. The door was opened, and there was a man, white with flakes, for it was beginning to snow, and he was pulling in a large box.

Mrs. Peterkin supposed it contained some of Elizabeth Eliza's purchases, so she ordered it to be pushed into the back parlor, and hastily called back her guests and the little boys into the other room. The little boys and the small cousins were sure they had seen Santa Claus himself.

Mr. Peterkin lighted the gas. The box was addressed to Elizabeth Eliza. It was from the lady from Philadelphia! She had gathered a hint from Elizabeth Eliza's letters that there was to be a Christmas tree, and had filled this box with all that would be needed.

It was opened directly. There was every kind of gilt hanging-thing, from gilt pea-pods to butterflies on springs. There were shining flags and lanterns, and bird-cages, and nests with birds sitting on them, baskets of fruit, gilt apples and bunches of grapes, and, at the bottom of the whole, a large box of candles and a box of Philadelphia bonbons!

Elizabeth Eliza and Solomon John could scarcely keep from screaming. The little boys and the small cousins knocked on the folding-doors to ask what was the matter.

Hastily Mr. Peterkin and the rest took out the things and hung them on the tree, and put on the candles.

When all was done, it looked so well that Mr. Peterkin exclaimed:

"Let us light the candles now, and send to invite all the neighbors tonight, and have the tree on Christmas Eve!"

And so it was that the Peterkins had their Christmas tree the day before, and on Christmas night could go and visit their neighbors.

Mrs. Goose's Wild Christmas

Miriam Clark Potter

One morning in December when Mrs. Goose went to her front door, there was a letter for her. It was written on birch-bark paper and tied around with green grass ribbon.

Mrs. Goose was so excited that her wings fluttered and trembled. She opened the envelope, sat down in her little rocking chair, and put on her glasses.

The letter was printed in queer, green, wiggly letters. It said:

"DEAR MRS. GOOSE,

Please come and spend Christmas with me in my

river home. I will fly by for you at five o'clock on Christmas Eve. Be ready to fly up and fly away with me.

Your flying cousin,

MRS. WILD-GOOSE-OF-THE-MARSHES."

"My, there are a lot of 'flys' in that letter," said Mrs. Goose, blinking. She got up from her rocking chair and said to herself, "I don't believe I know how to fly. I've been a tame goose for so long that I've forgotten."

She thought for a minute, and then she flapped her wings. "No, I haven't forgotten," she told herself.

Three-Ducks were coming over for a cup of hot clover tea at four o'clock. Mrs. Goose kept very busy till they came, tying up presents for her friends. Three yellow bow ties for Three-Ducks, a nice new tail comb for Mrs. Squirrel, and little currant cakes for Mr. Pig and the Pop-Rabbits and her other friends. "Don't open till Christmas," she wrote on them. "They can look at them when they have the big Animaltown Christmas Tree party," she planned. "But I won't be here!" Yes, she had decided to spend Christmas with her wild marsh cousin.

At four o'clock, she heard a quacking at the door, and she ran to let Three-Ducks in. "It's getting very cold and blowy," they told her, as they marched over to the fire. "We think it's going to snow," they said, as they warmed their wings.

"I hope it won't snow on Christmas Eve at five o'clock," Mrs. Goose told them, "because I am going away then."

"*Away?*" quacked Three-Ducks, looking at her.

"Yes, away; I am going to visit my cousin, Mrs. Wild-Goose," and she showed them the birch-bark letter.

"Oh, Mrs. Goose—you won't be here for Christmas —and our big Animaltown party," said Three-Ducks.

"No."

"Why—we'll miss you so much!"

"I'll miss you, too," said Mrs. Goose, getting the teapot.

"And you'll not like the way your cousin lives. She doesn't have a cozy home like yours! She sleeps in a wet river place."

Mrs. Goose poured the tea. "Yes, but she *is* my cousin," she told Three-Ducks. "Our mothers were sister geese. I have decided to go."

They drank their tea, and they talked some more about it, but Three-Ducks couldn't make Mrs. Goose change her mind. She was just determined to go on Christmas Eve; that was all there was about it.

On the day before Christmas, Mrs. Goose was very busy. She tied bright bunches of holly berries on her friends' presents. She packed a little bag with her long gray nightgown and funny white nightcap, and feather-brush. She swept her house and put it all in order. Then she put on her red shoes and her blue and lavender dress and bright red shawl and hat with parsley on it.

She looked at herself in the glass and said, "There I am. I look very handsome, really—I hope my cousin will be proud of me."

Tap—tap—tap. There were Three-Ducks at the door. They had come to see her off. *Scratch—scratch—*

[264]

scratch. That was Mrs. Squirrel. Then came Mr. Pig and Mr. Gobbler and the Pop-Rabbits. It was very exciting, coming to see Mrs. Goose fly off—just like waiting to see a balloon go up, or something. "Do you *know* how to fly?" asked Mrs. Squirrel. "Yes, I know," answered Mrs. Goose.

They all went outside to watch for Mrs. Wild-Goose.

The wind made little scurry-tracks in the snow, and there were gray clouds scudding over. "I wish she'd hurry," said Mrs. Goose, drawing her shawl closer around her. "I'm cold."

"I wish you'd change your mind," sighed Mrs. Squirrel. "I hate to think of your flying around loose in the sky somewhere. Don't go!!"

"Yes, I'm going," said Mrs. Goose, firmly.

"I don't believe her cousin is coming," Three-Ducks whispered. "It's five minutes past five already."

But just then there was a faraway honking sound. In a minute, a wild goose came into sight. She came nearer and nearer. She flew right over Mrs. Goose's chimney.

"There she is—good-by—" said Mrs. Goose, flapping her wings.

But there she stayed, right on the ground.

"Try again," said Three-Ducks.

She flapped and flapped, but she did not rise.

"Take off your clothes!" came a wild voice from the sky. "Throw off your bag! You are too-o-o heavy!" And there was a sound like laughter, cold laughter, with wind in it.

So Mrs. Goose took off her dress, and her shawl, and her hat, and threw her bag down on the ground. She flapped her wings again, and up she rose, with a great noise. As she rose, she kicked off her red shoes. They fell down and one of them whacked Mr. Pig on the nose.

"Good-by—Mrs. Goose—" Mr. Pig sneezed.

"Good-by," they all called.

"Good-by—" she answered them, as she rose higher and higher.

"There she goes, for her wild Christmas," said Three-Ducks. "I hope she'll have a good time." They gulped hard in their throats, because they missed her already. "We'd better take her things into the house, and lock the door, just as she told us to, and put the key under the mat. There she flies—over the pine treetops. And there are going to be lots of presents for her at the Christmas party tomorrow—and she won't be here to get them. She said she'd open them when she got back."

"Maybe she won't *get* back," sighed Mrs. Squirrel. "Maybe we'll never see her again." And they all began to cry a little, feeling so sad on Christmas Eve at quarter past five o'clock.

At seven o'clock, when Three-Ducks came back from a little visit at Mrs. Squirrel's house, there was a light shining from Mrs. Goose's window.

"We must go and look in," they said. "Who could be there? Mrs. Goose is away. We must go and see."

So they plopped over and peeked in the window.

There was Mrs. Goose with her wrapper and white nightcap on, warming her wings before the fire.

Tap—tap—tap at the door went Three-Ducks, with excited bills. They were *so* glad!

"Shhhhhh!" said Mrs. Goose, as she let them in. "Yes, I'm back. (Whisper.) Yes, my wings are tired. (*Please* whisper!) For my wild cousin is here—she's in my bed, sleeping. She's come to spend Christmas with me."

"But we thought you were going to spend Christmas with *her!*"

"I did spend two hours with her," said Mrs. Goose. "That was long enough. Yes, you were right, Three-Ducks. Her house is very cold, right by the river. Just frozen rattly reeds, lumps of ice, and wind blowing your feathers this way and that. One of my best tail feathers blew right out! She had a few wintergreen berries stuck around; we ate those. 'This is our Christmas dinner, really,' said my cousin. 'We'll have it today, instead of tomorrow. We'll spend Christmas flying, my tame cousin. You need practice. You fly very badly. We'll go far over those snow-covered hills.' "

"How cold and unpleasant," shivered Three-Ducks. "What did you say?"

"I said—'Now I've had a sort of a Christmas with you—a nice berry meal—please come back to my house with me, and see what Christmas there is like. We give presents to each other; we have a party and lots of dancing and laughing, and try to make each other happy and full of pleasant feelings.' And do you know—she had never heard of a party in a house beside a fire. She didn't know about giving presents! Awfully wild, I think. Well, I talked and talked, and after a while she said she would come."

"And she's here now—sleeping in your bed?" asked Three-Ducks. "Oh, do let us have a peek at her, please."

"Will you be very quiet? Will you put your feet down softly, and not quack?"

"Oh, yes; yes."

So Mrs. Goose lit a candle, and they stepped softly to the bedroom. She held the light up high, so they could see better.

But there was no one in the bed!

The covers were thrown back, as though someone had got out quickly, and there was one long feather on the blanket.

"Why—she's *gone,*" said Mrs. Goose, looking at the open window.

"She's flown away. You can't be wild, and she can't be tame," said Three-Ducks, wisely.

"Our mothers were sister geese," Mrs. Goose told them. "But *we* don't seem to belong in the same family."

"And you'll be here for the Christmas party, after all," laughed Three-Ducks.

*　　*　　*　　*　　*

And they had the happiest Christmas that they had ever had. Ragtag and Bobtail and Billy Squirrel and all the other animal children had some jolly little toys, and all the grown-up animals had great fun opening their own presents. They sang animal songs, and played games, and the refreshments were delicious. The tree was trimmed with little balls of cotton, strings of pink popcorn, and a few stars and candles.

Mrs. Goose was so happy that she got all mixed up: she dropped nuts into her tea instead of lemon, said "Happy Birthday" to Mr. Pig instead of "Merry Christmas," and when it was time to go home, she put her rubbers on her wings instead of on her feet. But no one cared, they were so glad to see her back again. "And you won't fly away again, will you?" Three-Ducks asked her.

And she said, "No. One wild Christmas is enough for me. Animaltown is where *I* belong, forever and ever!"

ACKNOWLEDGMENTS
AND
ABOUT THE AUTHORS

Acknowledgments

"CHRISTMAS PANTOMIME" is reprinted from *Jeremy* by Hugh Walpole, copyright, 1919, by Doubleday, Doran & Company, Inc.

"A MISERABLE, MERRY CHRISTMAS" is from *Boy On Horseback* by Lincoln Steffens. Reprinted by permission of Harcourt, Brace and Company, Inc.

"A CHRISTMAS CAROL" by G. K. Chesterton is reprinted from *Fifty Christmas Poems For Children* by Florence B. Hyett, by permission of D. Appleton-Century Company, New York.

"BORN IS THE KING OF ISRAEL" is reprinted from *Roller Skates* by Ruth Sawyer, copyright 1936, published by The Viking Press, Inc., New York.

"THE BIRTHDAY" by Margaret E. Sangster is reprinted by courtesy of the author and *Good Housekeeping*.

"THE CHRISTMAS MASQUERADE" is reprinted from *The Pot of Gold* by Mary E. Wilkins Freeman; and "SANTA CLAUS" is reprinted from *A Story Garden for Little Children* by Maud Lindsay, both by permission of Lothrop, Lee & Shepard Company.

"THE PETERKINS' CHRISTMAS TREE" is reprinted from *Peterkin Papers* by Lucretia P. Hale, by permission of Houghton Mifflin Company, Boston.

ACKNOWLEDGMENTS

"Mrs. Goose's Wild Christmas" is reprinted from *Mrs. Goose and Three-Ducks* by Miriam Clark Potter, copyright 1936, by Miriam Clark Potter, by permission of Frederick A. Stokes Company.

"The First New England Christmas" is reprinted from *Everyday Life in the Colonies* by Gertrude L. Stone and M. Grace Fickett, by permission of D. C. Heath and Company.

"Pegasus and the Star" by John Brangwyn was first published in *Child Life,* December, 1932, copyright 1932, Rand McNally & Co.

"Christmas Sheaves" by Nora Burglon is reprinted from *St. Nicholas* with the permission of the author.

"Christmas Gifts" and "Little Girl of Long Ago" by Marjorie Barrows; "Christmas in the Street of Memories" by Elizabeth Rhodes Jackson; "The Runaway Christmas Bus" by Florence Page Jaques; "Lord Octopus Went to the Christmas Fair" by Stella Mead; "A Christmas Gift for the General" by Jeannette Covert Nolan; "A Trade-About Christmas" by Frances Cavanah and "Sky-Fallen Peace" by Josephine E. Phillips are reprinted from *Child Life* with the permission of the authors.

"On Christmas Eve" is reprinted from *The Land of Never-Grow-Old* by Stella Mead, by permission of the author.

The translation of "The Stranger Child" by Count Franz Pocci and the adaptation of "The Christmas Rose" by Lizzie Deas are reprinted from *Good Stories for Great Holidays* by Frances Jenkins Olcott, by permission of Houghton, Mifflin Company, Boston.

About the Authors

Hans Christian Andersen, who lived in Denmark a hundred years ago, is still the world's best-loved writer of fairy tales. ("The Fir Tree," page 13.)

Marjorie Barrows, for many years the editor of *Child Life* magazine, has also written and compiled a number of children's books. These include *Two Hundred Best Poems for Boys and Girls* and such nursery favorites as *Muggins Mouse* and *Ezra the Elephant*. ("Little Girl of Long Ago," page 105; "Christmas Gifts," page 33.)

Phillips Brooks, famous clergyman and orator of the last century, is best remembered for his Christmas hymns. ("O Little Town of Bethlehem," page 58.)

Nora Burglon has given American boys and girls a vivid picture of child life in the Scandinavian countries in such books as *Children of the Soil* and *Sticks Across the Chimney*. ("Christmas Sheaves," page 81.)

Frances Hodgson Burnett, English-American author, has been beloved by three generations for such books as *Little Lord Fauntleroy*, *Sara Crewe*, and *The Secret Garden*. ("Behind the White Brick," page 234.)

Frances Cavanah, author of *Boyhood Adventures of Our Presidents*, *Children of the White House*, and other books, was formerly the associate editor of *Child Life*. ("A Trade-About Christmas," page 130.)

G. K. CHESTERTON, one of the most versatile of English writers, died in 1936. He was known both for his *Father Brown* detective stories and his critical work. ("A Christmas Carol," page 31.)

LOU CRANDALL, an editor of children's textbooks, was formerly on the staff of *Compton's Pictured Encyclopedia*. ("Yuletide Customs in Many Lands," page 61.)

CHARLES DICKENS, seventy years after his death, is still one of the world's favorite authors. Listening to his *Christmas Carol* on the radio has become an annual Christmas custom for millions of Americans. ("Tiny Tim's Christmas," page 6.)

M. GRACE FICKETT was co-author of *Everyday Life in the Colonies,* which has been popular with school children for the last thirty-five years. ("The First New England Christmas," page 95.)

MARY E. WILKINS FREEMAN was a New England writer, noted for her short stories for adults. Among her books were *A New England Nun* and *A Humble Romance*—for grown people—and *The Pot of Gold* and *Young Lucretia*—for children. At one time she was secretary to Oliver Wendell Holmes. ("The Christmas Masquerade," page 199.)

LUCRETIA P. HALE was the grandniece of Nathan Hale and the sister of Edward Everett Hale. She gained fame in her own right and won the gratitude of thousands of American children with her solemnly hilarious *Peterkin Papers* and *The Last of the Peterkins*. ("The Peterkins' Christmas Tree," page 253.)

ELIZABETH RHODES JACKSON is a contributor to magazines. She lives in the section of Boston which is the setting of so many of her stories. ("Christmas in the Street of Memories," page 166.)

FLORENCE PAGE JAQUES is author of *Canoe Country* and *The Geese Fly High* and is a contributor to magazines. ("The Runaway Christmas Bus," page 215.)

ABOUT THE AUTHORS

MAUD LINDSAY, well-known kindergartner, is author of *The Storyland Tree, The Choosing Book,* and other books for small children. ("Santa Claus, a Wonder Story," page 231.)

STELLA MEAD is the popular English author of *Princes and Fairies, The Land of Never-Grow-Old,* and other books. ("Lord Octopus Went to the Christmas Fair," page 251; "On Christmas Eve," page 229.)

CLEMENT CLARKE MOORE, nineteenth-century scholar and teacher, is chiefly remembered for a poem he wrote for his own children—the famous " 'Twas the Night Before Christmas." (Page 3.)

JEANNETTE COVERT NOLAN is the author of *The Young Douglas, Red Hugh of Ireland,* and other books for older boys and girls. She has contributed to magazines. ("A Christmas Gift for the General," page 107.)

JOSEPHINE E. PHILLIPS is a contributor to magazines. She lives in Marietta, Ohio, and the early history of her state has furnished the background for many of her stories. ("Sky-Fallen Peace," page 120.)

MIRIAM CLARK POTTER is the author of *The Giant of Apple Pie Hill, Mrs. Goose and Three-Ducks,* and other books for younger children. ("Mrs. Goose's Wild Christmas," page 262.)

MARGARET E. SANGSTER is a popular novelist and contributor to leading adult magazines. Among her books are *The Stars Come Close* and *Singing on the Road.* ("The Birthday," page 38.)

RUTH SAWYER won the Newbery Medal in 1937 for *Roller Skates,* a story based on her own childhood. She is a well-known storyteller and author of *This Way to Christmas* and other books for boys and girls. ("Born is the King of Israel," page 152.)

LINCOLN STEFFENS, an important American journalist, died in 1936. His *Autobiography* was a best seller a few years ago, and that portion of it published as a juvenile under the title, *Boy on Horseback,* was popular with boys and girls. ("A Miserable, Merry Christmas," page 144.)

ABOUT THE AUTHORS

GERTRUDE L. STONE was co-author of *Everyday Life in the Colonies,* a book popular in schools since 1905. ("The First New England Christmas," page 95.)

HUGH WALPOLE, one of England's most distinguished novelists, has told us the story of his own boyhood in *Jeremy.* "Christmas Pantomime" is a selection from this book. (Page 66.)